From the Diary of Maeve Elliott

Ever since birth, my twin granddaughters, Summer and Scarlet, have been total opposites. Scarlet is a whirlwind, a blur of color and energy with a wild side. And then there's sensible Summer, who has never given me a sleepless night. Until now.

The tabloid photo caused quite a stir. After all, we least expected it from her. She knows well the demands that come with being an Elliott. But life, as Summer and I know, doesn't always go according to plan.

Her Zeke is charming and sweet and—I'm not too old to notice—very handsome. Beyond that, he and Summer are nothing alike. But that's what my parents said about me and Patrick—fifty-seven years ago. No, Summer is changing, searching… and for the first time I see a sparkle in her Irish-green eyes. Could it be love?

Dear Reader,

Thanks for taking time out of your hectic life to pick up and enjoy a Silhouette Desire novel. We have six outstanding reads for you this month, beginning with the latest in our continuity series, THE ELLIOTTS. Anna DePalo's *Cause for Scandal* will thrill you with a story of a quiet twin who takes on her identical sister's persona and falls for a dynamic hero. Look for her sister to turn the tables next month.

The fabulous Kathie DeNosky wraps up her ILLEGITIMATE HEIRS trilogy with the not-to-be-missed *Betrothed for the Baby*—a compelling engagement-of-convenience story. We welcome back Mary Lynn Baxter to Silhouette Desire with *Totally Texan,* a sensual story with a Lone Star hero to drool over. WHAT HAPPENS IN VEGAS...is perhaps better left there unless you're the heroine of Katherine Garbera's *Her High-Stakes Affair*—she's about to make the biggest romantic wager of all.

Also this month are two stories of complex relationships. Cathleen Galitz's *A Splendid Obsession* delves into the romance between an ex-model with a tormented past and the hero who finds her all the inspiration he needs. And Nalini Singh's *Secrets in the Marriage Bed* finds a couple on the brink of separation with a reason to fight for their marriage thanks to a surprise pregnancy.

Here's hoping this month's selection of Silhouette Desire novels bring you all the enjoyment you crave.

Happy reading!

Melissa Jeglinski

Melissa Jeglinski
Senior Editor
Silhouette Desire

Please address questions and book requests to:
Silhouette Reader Service
U.S.: 3010 Walden Ave., P.O. Box 1325, Buffalo, NY 14269
Canadian: P.O. Box 609, Fort Erie, Ont. L2A 5X3

ANNA DePALO

Cause for Scandal

Published by Silhouette Books
America's Publisher of Contemporary Romance

For Amy Liu and Gloria Miller,
two friends that I couldn't do without.
Acknowledgment
Special thanks and acknowledgment are given to
Anna DePalo for her contribution to THE ELLIOTTS series.

 SILHOUETTE BOOKS

ISBN 0-373-76711-0

CAUSE FOR SCANDAL

Visit Silhouette Books at www.eHarlequin.com

Printed in U.S.A.

Books by Anna DePalo

Silhouette Desire

Having the Tycoon's Baby #1530
Under the Tycoon's Protection #1643
Tycoon Takes Revenge #1697
Cause for Scandal #1711

ANNA DePALO

A lifelong book lover, Anna discovered that she was a writer at heart when she realized that not everyone travels around with a full cast of characters in their head. She has lived in Italy and England, learned to speak French, graduated from Harvard, earned graduate degrees in political science and law, forgotten how to speak French and married her own dashing hero.

Anna has been an intellectual-property lawyer in New York City. She loves traveling, reading, writing, old movies, chocolate and Italian (which she hasn't forgotten how to speak, thanks to her extended Italian family). She's thrilled to be writing for Silhouette. Readers are invited to surf to www.desireauthors.com and can also visit her at www.annadepalo.com.

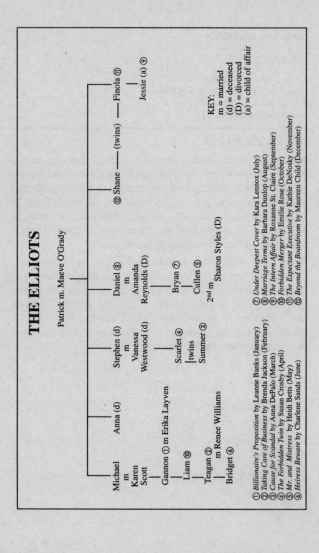

THE ELLIOTS

Patrick m. Maeve O'Grady

Michael
m
Karen
Scott

Anna (d)

Gannon ① m Erika Layven

Liam ⑩

Teagan ②
m Renee Williams

Bridget ⑥

Stephen (d)
m
Vanessa
Westwood (d)

Scarlet ④ ⎰
     ⎱ twins
Summer ③

Daniel ⑧
m
Amanda
Reynolds (D)

Bryan ⑦

Cullen ⑤

2ⁿᵈ m
Sharon Styles (D)

② Shane —— (twins) —— Finola ⑪

Jessie (a) ⑨

KEY:
m = married
(d) = deceased
(D) = divorced
(a) = child of affair

① *Billionaire's Proposition* by Leanne Banks (January)
② *Taking Care of Business* by Brenda Jackson (February)
③ *Cause for Scandal* by Anna DePalo (March)
④ *The Forbidden Twin* by Susan Crosby (April)
⑤ *Mr. and Mistress* by Heidi Betts (May)
⑥ *Heiress Beware* by Charlene Sands (June)
⑦ *Under Deepest Cover* by Kara Lennox (July)
⑧ *Marriage Terms* by Barbara Dunlop (August)
⑨ *The Intern Affair* by Roxanne St. Claire (September)
⑩ *Forbidden Merger* by Emilie Rose (October)
⑪ *The Expectant Executive* by Kathie DeNosky (November)
⑫ *Beyond the Boardroom* by Maureen Child (December)

One

She needed this interview. Her career depended on it. Her *plan* depended on it. And, as far as she could see, all that stood in her way were a few burly security guards, her lack of a backstage pass and close to twenty thousand shrieking Zeke Woodlow fans.

Summer looked at Zeke on stage. Even from her seat twelve rows back, his charisma was palpable. His blue jeans and black T-shirt outlined a lean and muscular physique. He wore his dark-brown hair longish, touching the collar of his shirt, and tousled, emphasizing his bad-boy image.

It was his gorgeous face, however, that really got

his fans going. Summer itched to capture that arrest-ing face with her camera.

Just then Zeke seemed to look right at her, and Summer held her breath. The connection lasted just an instant, but she felt his intensity down to the tips of her toes.

She only expelled a breath when he looked away.

No doubt about it. Zeke Woodlow's sex appeal was potent.

Not that he was her type, of course.

She looked down at the round, two-carat, bril-liant-cut diamond engagement ring on her hand.

Not at all.

As she was again jostled by fans, she bit back a sigh of impatience and looked around.

Madison Square Garden. One of New York City's premier venues. Host to political conventions, site for countless sporting events and witness to history. Frank Sinatra, Elvis Presley, The Rolling Stones, Elton John, Bruce Springsteen…and now Zeke Woodlow—Grammy winner, rock sensation and current "it" boy of the music world, whose latest CD, *Falling For You,* had gone diamond, selling over ten million copies.

Summer had all the vital information on Zeke. She knew that he'd grown up in New York but now lived in a Beverly Hills mansion, that he'd become famous for his sexy lyrics and that he'd helped start

Musicians for a Cure, which had led to his headlining a Madison Square Garden concert series to benefit cancer research.

But, while she had all the facts, she didn't have access, and unfortunately she had her heart set on getting an interview with Zeke for *The Buzz.* She'd been thinking for months about how to win a promotion at work. Her paternal grandfather, Patrick Elliott, believed even relatives had to work their way up within the family publishing empire.

So, when she'd come home one day and spotted an advertisement for Musicians for a Cure among her mail, she knew she'd found her ticket to moving up from lowly copy editor to trusted reporter. An interview with Zeke Woodlow would be just right for *The Buzz,* which was locked in a fierce battle not only with its closest rival in format, *Entertainment Weekly,* but also with other Elliott magazines. Patrick Elliott had declared that the head of whichever magazine in the family empire was the most profitable by the end of the year would become the new CEO of EPH— Elliott Publication Holdings—when he stepped down.

Now, clutching her notepad and pen, she shifted from one foot to the other. She'd come to the concert straight from work and she felt uncomfortable. Her toes in her chunky-heeled boots had been stepped on more times than she could count. Her pinstriped pants were perfect for the office but were too warm and out of place among a sea of jeans. Her turtleneck felt similarly tight and hot in the heat generated by thousands of swaying, dancing, jiggling bodies.

Around her, the audience seemed to move like a wave, swaying toward the stage and back, caressing the outer perimeter of Zeke Woodlow's spotlight.

Because she was just a copy editor, she knew Zeke's publicist would have laughed in her face if she'd asked for an exclusive interview. But she hoped if she got close to Zeke himself, she could convince him to talk to her. After all, she was ambitious, articulate and musically aware, and she worked for *The Buzz*—even if her position didn't qualify her for a backstage press pass.

When Zeke finished the song he was singing, the crowd went wild. He joked with the audience, his sexy voice filling the arena and dancing across her skin like an intimate caress.

"More?" he asked, his voice deep and smooth as silk, teasing the crowd.

The audience hooted and hollered in response.

"I can't hear you," he said, cupping his hand to his ear.

The crowd roared.

"All right!" Zeke motioned to the band behind him, then slung the strap of an electric guitar over his shoulder. The music struck up, and Zeke started crooning one of his biggest hits, a ballad called "Beautiful in My Arms."

As he sang about making love beneath waving palm trees, with the humid night air pressing around, Summer felt herself being seduced right along with the rest of the crowd, lulled into a magical moment. Only when the song faded away was the spell broken, and, even then, it took a few seconds before she shook herself and told herself to stop being ridiculous.

She had to remember she was here for one purpose and one purpose only, and it wasn't to become another of Zeke Woodlow's ardent admirers.

Thirty minutes later, when the concert had ended and the crowd was making for the exits, she pushed through the throng, intent on getting backstage. Unfortunately, her progress was halted by a tall and tough-looking security guard.

"Excuse me," she said, "I'd like to get backstage."

The guard peered down at her, his eyes catching on her ring for an instant, his arms folded. "Right. You and a few thousand other people."

"I'm a member of the press," she said. She invested her voice with the same tone that she'd heard hundreds of times from the headmistress of the private girls' school that she'd attended along with her identical twin, Scarlet.

"Let's see your backstage pass."

"I don't have one. You see—"

But Mr. Hefty-and-Imperturbable had already

started shaking his head. "No pass, no access. It's that simple."

She wanted to say, "Can we talk about this?" But since she doubted that would work, she fished in her handbag for a business card. She held one up. "See? I'm a staff member—" she didn't bother identifying *which* staff member "—at *The Buzz*. You've heard of *The Buzz*, haven't you?"

Mr. Hefty just glanced from the business card to her, not bothering to take the card from her. "Like I said, only authorized persons are permitted backstage."

Argh. She should have been prepared for this.

"Fine," she said in exasperation, trying one last gambit, "but don't blame me when heads roll because Zeke Woodlow lost his chance at an interview with one of the leading entertainment magazines in the country."

The guard merely quirked a brow.

Turning on her heel, she marched away with her head held high. At school, Ms. Donaldson would have been proud.

All right, she thought, so she wasn't going to get to interview Zeke in his dressing room. She knew he had to leave the Garden sometime, though, and when he did, she'd be waiting for him. She hadn't spent close to three hours getting shoved and poked by his fans for nothing. She *needed* this interview.

An hour later, however, she felt as if she'd been huddling in the chilly, damp March night forever, and she started to ask herself how much she needed this interview. She was tired, hungry and wanted to go home.

She started fishing around in her purse for a breath mint—anything edible, frankly—until a commotion caused her to look up and notice that Zeke had emerged.

Unfortunately, he was surrounded by handlers and security personnel. Despite that, she ran forward, knowing she had only a few moments before he ducked into the limousine that had pulled up. "Zeke! Mr. Woodlow!"

Just then, the space around Zeke became frenetic. Paparazzi flashbulbs went off, and some girls started screaming and jumping up and down.

Her forward progress came to a halt as she collided with a brick wall—or, more precisely, she realized as she looked up, the blue-clad form of one of New York's finest. She took an involuntary step back as the police officer—one of several near the limo, she now noticed—blocked her way.

"Step back," he ordered.

Looking over the officer's shoulder, she noticed Zeke duck into the car, and her shoulders slumped.

Four hours, twenty-seven minutes and twenty-plus songs. And now, finally, defeat.

She felt like wailing in frustration. As if on cue, a raindrop hit her cheek, then another. She looked up, grimaced and then made a beeline for the taxi stand on Seventh Avenue. Once it started raining in earnest, she knew there wouldn't be an empty cab in sight.

Twenty-five minutes later, she reached the Upper West Side townhouse owned by her grandparents and used by them as a secondary residence.

When she got to the top floor, where she and Scarlet had living quarters, her sister padded out of her room to greet her. "Well, how'd it go?" asked Scarlet, who was dressed in red silk pajamas.

Taking in her sister's sleepwear, she thought again that she and Scarlet couldn't be more different, despite being identical twins. Scarlet was known as flamboyant and wild and crazy, while she was thought of as sensible and methodical.

"Horribly," she responded, plopping down on the couch and unzipping her boots. She wiggled her toes in relief. "I don't know what ever made me think I could land this interview with Zeke. I couldn't even get near him! The guy has better security than the pope and the president combined."

She summarized the events of the evening for Scarlet, then shrugged. "It was a crazy plan to begin with, but now I need another career-making scheme. Any ideas?"

"That's it?" Scarlet asked disbelievingly. "Just like that—" she snapped her fingers "—you're giving up on Zeke?"

"Not just like that," she said, snapping her fingers

right back. "Haven't you been listening to anything I've said?"

"Isn't there one more concert scheduled for tomorrow night? You've still got a shot at getting the interview."

"Scar, hello?" She was used to administering a dose of reality to counter her sister's exuberance. "There isn't going to be an interview."

Scarlet rested her hands on her hips. "Well, not with you dressed like *that* there isn't."

She looked down at her clothes. "What's wrong with the way I'm dressed?"

"You're dressed like a nun." Gesturing with one hand, Scarlet added, "You're practically covered from head to toe."

"It's cold outside," she said defensively. "Besides, are you seriously suggesting I'd get anywhere by showing some cleavage?"

"Well, it can't hurt."

"Right, and I suppose it would help if I borrowed a few things from your closet," she said dryly.

Her sister's eyes lit up. "Now there's an idea."

Scarlet's love of fashion was well known. She often sketched designs and sometimes made her own clothes, and Summer admired her for it, though her own taste in clothes was more sedate.

"Forget it."

"It's perfect! Why didn't I think of it before?"

"What?"

"The way to get past Zeke Woodlow's security. Dress up as a rock groupie. They're always allowing attractive women backstage."

"Why?"

Scarlet sighed in exasperation. "Summer, sometimes I swear you were born with the mindset of a fifty-year-old. Why do you think? Sometimes it's sex, sometimes it's fawning attention and sometimes it's just positive publicity, because the women will later gush to reporters about talking to a rock star."

"Oh, please! You want me to dress like an airhead? I'm looking to inspire respect as a reporter, not lust as a bimbette."

Scarlet spun on her heel. "Come on! Tomorrow night you're going to be dressed to seduce. The serious part can come *after* you get your stiletto in the door. You're going to a rock concert, not doing an interview at the United Nations."

Summer sighed, but she got up and trudged after her twin. She could easily imagine what Scarlet had in mind—and *that* was the problem.

As one stiletto-heeled foot hit the pavement, Summer steeled herself for what lay ahead. She looked up at the Garden as she emerged from the cab and chanted Scarlet's advice from earlier.

Release your inner goddess.... Release your inner goddess....

She kept up the chant as she walked toward the entrance to the Garden.

At five o'clock, she'd left her desk at work and taken the elevator at EPH's headquarters down to *Charisma*'s offices, where her sister was employed. Scarlet had helped her dress in the clothes that they'd pulled from the closet last night, then had applied her makeup and styled her hair.

Summer didn't have to wonder how she looked. She'd stared at her image in the full-length mirror at *Charisma*'s offices long enough.

Dramatic. Sexy. In short, a different person. Her lips twisted wryly. A different person who happened to look a lot like Scarlet herself. Not surprisingly, of course, since she was dressed in Scarlet's clothes, and Scarlet—whether by design or subconsciously—appeared to think that *sexy* meant a lot like the look she herself wore when hitting the town hard.

Summer touched her hair. It was down and loose, its curls cascading past her shoulders.

Beneath her short, belted pea coat, she wore a black suede skirt that ended above the knee and black boots that ended right below. If Scarlet was to be believed, knees were sexy.

Her deep-red top plunged low, revealing tantalizing cleavage, and her face was made-up. Normally she favored a natural look, using matte lipstick with just a hint of color. But tonight, her lips were a dark red and had a lovely sheen due to the smattering of gold dust in her lipstick.

Apparently, gold of twenty-three karats or higher was edible. Who'd have known? Certainly not her. But as assistant fashion editor at *Charisma*—EPH's answer to *Vogue*—Scarlet was in a position to know.

As she walked into the Garden, Summer looked down at her ringless hand. There was no telltale pale band on her skin to give her away.

Her sister had insisted that she leave her engagement ring at home. When she'd protested, Scarlet had taken her hand and tugged at the ring herself.

"Don't be ridiculous, Summer," her sister had said. "How do you expect to impersonate a rock groupie?"

"What's the ring got to do with it?" she'd shot back, trying to pull her hand from Scarlet's grasp.

"Haven't we been over this? Groupies are allowed backstage because they're young, sexy and *single*. Are you going to go to all this trouble just to be done in by a ring?"

In the end, she'd let Scarlet take the ring. But the whole thing still didn't sit well with her. It felt as if she were being disloyal to John.

That feeling was ridiculous, of course. Tonight wasn't a date. She just happened to be trying to lure a rock star to do an interview by using some sex appeal. What the heck was wrong with that?

In fact, she had almost convinced herself. Almost.

She thought about John again. He'd be returning from his business trip soon—which was a good thing, since they had a wedding to plan.

She was a meticulous planner and list keeper, and getting engaged at twenty-five put her right on target as far as the five-year plan that she'd drawn up for herself.

It read like this: twenty-five, become engaged and rise to full reporter status at *The Buzz*; twenty-six, get married; twenty-eight, make name for self as hotshot entertainment reporter; thirty, rise to management position at *The Buzz* and become pregnant.

So far, so good. It helped, of course, that John had his own five-year plan. It was one of the things that had helped her pick him from the field of men that she used to date and that she had eventually winnowed down to The One.

Like her, John was serious and ambitious. At twenty-nine, he was already a partner at his advertising firm and had an impressive clientele that required him to fly around the country on business.

He was her perfect complement, and by this time next year she'd be Mrs. John Harlan. After nine months of dating, John had popped the question to her over a romantic dinner on Valentine's Day.

The perfection of the proposal had been the last proof she'd needed that she was making the right decision: she'd been thinking that Valentine's Day would be the right time to get engaged, but the comportment-school grad in her had been too polite to drop hints. But then John had gone ahead and proposed.

So what if, late at night, alone in bed, she experienced the occasional twinge of unease? Weren't all brides supposed to be nervous?

Turning her attention to the concert as it finally started, she soon found herself swept up in the dreamy mood that she'd fallen into the night before.

If she'd been tempted to dismiss last night's concert as a fluke, this time there could be no denying Zeke Woodlow's power as a performer and, more importantly, his ability to affect her.

Occasionally, she stopped to write in a small notebook, searching for the right adjectives to describe his performance and his electric effect on the audience.

When Zeke got to "Beautiful in My Arms," she again felt magically transported and as if he were singing just for her. It was almost like the feeling she'd experienced in one other situation—when she'd let herself do something totally out of character….

She jerked her mind back from the direction of her thoughts. No sense thinking about that now. It was her little secret. Tonight was about getting a job done.

This time with some luck—and insider tips from a coworker at *The Buzz*—she managed to sneak out of the arena at the end of the concert and locate the hallway that led to the performers' dressing rooms.

She had her coat unbuttoned—as Scarlet had said, "Show them the goods"—and a small suede handbag dangled from one hand.

She steeled herself as she approached the first burly security detail standing guard. *You can do this.*

She flashed him a breezy smile, noticing his eyes did a quick dart up and down as she approached. His face relaxed a fraction, male appreciation replacing cold stoniness.

Well, well. Scarlet was right.

Feeling suddenly empowered, she kept her smile in place and flicked him a coy look. "I'm here to see Zeke. He said to look him up when he was in New York."

"Did he?"

She nodded, standing close. "I spoke to Marty—" she'd made sure she knew the name of Zeke's manager, since, if you were going to lie through your teeth, there was no sense in being wrong "—and he said to come right up after the concert."

"You know Marty?"

"Only for the last five cities. I've seen Zeke play in L.A., Chicago, Boston…." She trailed off, then added significantly, "We've always had a great time."

Mr. Burly nodded over his shoulder. "Third door on the left."

That was it? She felt like crying with relief. Instead, she smiled and said, "Thanks."

She thought she could get used to life as an auburn-haired bombshell. She felt liberated, almost reckless.

In front of Zeke's door, she took a steadying breath and knocked.

"Come in," said a male voice through the door.

Turning the doorknob, she stepped inside the softly lit dressing room.

From the other side of the room, his voice reached her. "I've been waiting for you."

His voice went through her like a heady shot of vodka. Deep, sexy, rich and vibrant, it was even more potent up close and personal than it was on stage.

His back stayed turned to her as he picked up a cell phone from a nearby table and pushed some buttons. "I'll be ready to leave for the hotel in about ten minutes. Is that okay with you, Marty?"

She could see he was still dressed in the black jeans and T-shirt that he'd worn on stage. His tight rear end was nicely defined beneath the denim, and the cotton of his shirt stretched across his muscular back and shoulders.

She cleared her throat. "I'm not Marty."

He swung around and stopped, staring at her.

His face was striking. Good-looking, yes, but also

compelling. And then there were the eyes. Oh, Lord, his eyes. They were as blue and fathomless as the ocean. She'd have said his face tended to harshness if it were not for them. Despite his reputation in the press for being somewhat surly, he had sweet eyes.

With the part of her brain that still functioned, she noticed he remained motionless. Was it just her imagination or was he as dumbstruck as she was?

"Yeah," he drawled finally, "I can see you're definitely not Marty. So who are you?"

Two

The notes of the song drifted through Zeke's mind again. It was the same song that sounded in his head whenever he dreamed of *her*. It would linger tantalizingly at the edges of his memory when he awoke, but dissipate into nothingness before he could grasp it, write it down and make it his own.

This time, though, the notes of the song sounded more clearly. It was as if the woman standing in front of him were calling them forth. She even looked like the woman in the photograph—the woman of his dreams. She was slender but curvaceous, and had long, auburn hair, though a shade or two lighter than the woman in the picture. And, he'd recognize those astonishing green eyes anywhere.

The major difference was that the woman in the anonymous photograph that he'd purchased at a street fair was dressed as a Greek goddess, while this one was certainly twenty-first century and doubtless a rock groupie at that. He didn't know who the photographer or the subject of the photograph was, but he did have one hint: the photo was called "Daphne at Play," according to the handwritten inscription across the bottom of its white matte frame.

Awareness stirred within him, and his muscles tightened. Whatever it was about this woman, she called to him. In his dreams, he'd imagined her hair splayed across his bed, her arms and legs wrapped around him, drawing him in.

Feeling himself grow hot, he asked brusquely, "You didn't answer my question. What's your name?"

Her eyes darted away before returning to his. "C-Caitlin."

He released the breath that he hadn't known he was holding. So, she wasn't Daphne. Still, he couldn't resist asking, "Have you done any modeling?"

Her brows drew together. "No."

"Well, you should consider it." Definitely not Daphne.

She raised her brows. "Really?"

"Really." He gave her a slow, appreciative smile

as he walked toward her. "You've got the body and face for it. And your eyes are unusual…captivating." He'd often wondered if the pale green eyes of the woman in his photograph had been real or a trick of lighting or computer technology.

"I could say the same thing about you."

He laughed. She was bewitching. He realized she must be one of those rock groupies that Marty sometimes sent backstage after a concert. Girls clamored for access to rock stars like him, and Marty thought it was good PR for him to appear accessible to some extent.

If Caitlin was the key to unlocking his creativity—and, hell, even if she wasn't—he knew he had to get to know her better. He'd never experienced such a profound connection with someone so fast. She was nearly the living embodiment of his fantasies.

He gestured to a couch. "Have a seat." He looked around. "Do you want a drink?"

"Th-thanks."

He quirked a brow. Made her nervous, did he? "To the seat or the drink?"

He watched in fascination as a telltale flush rose from the tops of her breasts to her face. "Yes to both," she said as walked over and sat on the couch, dropping her coat and handbag beside her.

"Beer okay?"

"Yes, thank you."

Turning away to pull two beers from a small fridge and pop the caps off, he puzzled over her reaction. Usually, women were all too ready to throw themselves at him in situations like this. Caitlin, however, was the picture of reserved politeness.

Surprisingly, he found he was turned on by it. He gave himself a mental shake. He needed to get a grip. Her resemblance to Daphne was muddying his mind.

He handed her a beer as he sat down next to her. She looked as if she wasn't sure what to do with it for a second, then, after watching him take a swig, delicately tipped the bottle to her lips and took a sip.

He felt that sip straight down to his groin and shifted. The room felt as if it were getting hotter and smaller by the second.

Still not looking at him, she quickly took another swallow of beer, causing even more foam to appear near the top of the bottle.

He smiled. "Didn't anyone ever teach you how to drink from a beer bottle?"

"I'm doing it wrong?"

He touched his bottle to hers. "Yeah," he said with mock gravity. "Look at the foam that's forming."

She tilted her bottle to the side for a better look. "Oh."

"Watch," he commanded. "Don't create any suction. Part your lips just a little and don't cover the whole opening." He brought the bottle to his lips and drank deeply. He prayed the cold beer would help cool him down.

She raised the bottle to her lips and imitated him.

"That's right," he said.

When she lowered the bottle, she looked at him, and he knew he wanted to kiss her. Her lips were pouty and red but still had an innocence to them.

In fact, though she was dressed provocatively, something didn't seem to fit. He could have sworn she was more pearls and cashmere than leather and spandex.

"Tell me about you," he said.

"What would you like to know?"

Everything. "Did you like the concert?"

"Yes. I liked hearing you sing 'Beautiful in My Arms.'"

"Did you?" He eyed her. It was the song he'd written on the day he'd purchased "Daphne at Play." "What do you like about it?"

She shifted, her gaze falling away from his. "It's just…nice."

"Just…nice?"

"Magical. It makes me think about—"

"Making love?" he joked.

Her gaze jerked to his. "No."

He sobered. "I'm kidding. You know all the stuff that's in there about making love under the palm trees?" At her nod, he said, "It seems to make a lot of people think about sex."

When she broke into a smile, he sank fast.

"No," she said slowly, "it makes me think about holding tight to one special person—the person you want to cling to on the darkest days."

Lord, she surprised him. Most people stopped at the sex part, but then most people weren't straight out of his fantasies.

"Do you usually let strange women into your dressing room?" she asked suddenly, then looked horrified the minute the words had left her mouth.

He fought a smile. "Sometimes," he admitted. "My manager seems to think my being accessible to fans to some extent is good for PR."

"Is that why you're here now?"

He shrugged. "It's part of the job. I flirt and play nice. Usually the women will turn around afterward and gush about meeting Zeke Woodlow. It keeps a nice, positive buzz going out there among the public and the press."

She nodded.

He couldn't believe he was being this honest with her, but she had the type of face—classically beautiful and innocent—that spoke to him. He just found it easy to tell her things. Marty, he knew, would be wincing right now.

"Which part of your job do you like the most?" she asked.

"The songwriting."

Her eyes widened a fraction. "Not the performing?"

"No," he said curtly. She had a knack for homing in on sensitive subjects, he'd give her that.

Clearing his throat, he nodded at her beer. "Drink up."

She took another sip.

He took another swig himself before offering a small explanation. "The concerts are just icing on the cake."

"Isn't it a little unusual for singers to write their own songs these days?"

"Rare," he concurred.

She looked around. "What about the parties? Don't you have an after-party to go to right now?"

"Yeah, but I prefer hiding out in here with you."

Her head swung back toward him. "Oh."

It was true, he realized. She radiated an aura of sweetness and purity that was all too rare in his world. "Sometimes I skip the parties, especially when I've got a busy schedule the next day."

"What do you do when there aren't any parties?"

There was always a party somewhere for someone like him, he wanted to say. Instead, he admitted, "Finagle an invitation from some staff member to a family dinner."

Her answering smile lit up her face.

They stared at each other until her smile slowly faded.

He felt the urge to kiss her rise again.

He started to lift his hand to her face when a knock sounded at the door.

Damn.

"Who is it?" he demanded.

One of the tech guys for the band stuck his head around the door. "Car's here. Marty wanted me to let you know. He's already left for the hotel."

He stood. "Right. Ten minutes."

With a quick look from him to Caitlin and back, the tech guy said, "Great" and then shut the door.

Zeke reached for Caitlin's beer while she stood up. Their fingers brushed as he took the bottle from her, sending a bolt of awareness shooting through him. From the look in her eyes, she felt it, too.

"Do you want to leave with me?" he asked.

Tell him, tell him. Tell him that you're here to get an interview.

Instead, Summer heard herself say, "Okay."

He looked satisfied. "Great."

When she'd walked into the room, some instinct that it was too early to blurt her true purpose had made her give him her middle name—Caitlin—when he'd asked. After that, it had been a quick and easy slide to the point of no return. He obviously thought she was a fan, and the more time passed, the harder it got for her to correct his misinterpretation.

Since she'd walked into the dressing room, she'd

been hit with an awareness of him that was powerful and overwhelming. At first, she'd been nervous and jittery, then they'd slid into the type of personal conversation that happened between people who'd known each other forever and a day.

But the strange thing was, she *did* feel as if she knew him. Maybe that feeling was due to all the research that she'd done on him, or maybe it was due to going to his concerts.

Nevertheless, looking at him now—at his blue, blue eyes, chiseled features, broad shoulders and muscled physique—she couldn't stop her heart from thudding or the shivers that chased over her skin.

She might feel as if she'd known him forever and a day, but her body still clamored for a carnal knowledge that was more than the illusion of remembrances.

Zeke picked up her coat and bag from the sofa. After giving her the handbag, he held her coat for her.

The gesture both surprised and pleased her. Who'd have thought a rock sensation like him would have manners worthy of Ms. Donaldson's comportment school class?

Turning, she slid her arms into the coat sleeves. When he released his hold on the collar, his hand brushed her neck, and heat zipped through her. He had an intoxicating effect on her, and she found that she didn't want it to stop.

Turning back to him, she gave him a bright smile.

"Ready?" he asked, reaching over to pull a leather jacket off a hook.

She nodded. At some point—soon, very soon—she knew she'd have to tell him that she was a reporter looking for an interview. In the meantime, though, she could buy herself some time to find the right opening for that revelation.

Zeke led the way down a corridor and to an area behind the concert stage. Bodyguards and handlers soon joined them, one of them opening a door that led outside, where she was hit by a blast of March cold air.

Looking around, she realized they were still in an enclosed area, though the driveway sloped down to the street. "Where are we?" she asked.

He must have noticed her shivering, because he asked, "Cold?" He put an arm around her as a limo pulled up.

She shivered again, though not just from the cold.

As he glanced down at her, the corners of his lips tilted upward. "To answer your question, this is the 'secret' exit out of here. The driveway leads down to a parking area for loading and unloading equipment. Both the driveway and the parking area have limited public access."

"It's not the way you left last night," she blurted, then felt her face turn hot with embarrassment.

He grinned. "Watching, were you?"

"Maybe." Standing pressed against him, she was

acutely aware of the heat emanating from him. Traitorously, her body wanted only to snuggle closer.

"Last night, I left through the suites and clubs entrance. I went up to some of the private boxes after the concert in order to thank some of the big donors to the event." He winked. "It pays off in future fundraising efforts."

"Oh." In her naiveté, she'd just assumed most stars left through the lofty-sounding suites and clubs entrance. Now she realized that catching sight of his departure last night had been pure luck.

"Of course," he said, "it had the added benefit of throwing off some of the fans and paparazzi." He nodded at the limo that had pulled up in front of them. "Once the car hits the street outside, don't be surprised if there are photographers trying to hold up high-powered lenses to the tinted car windows."

"Sounds awful." Not only did it sound awful, she knew it *was* awful. Though her life was nothing like Zeke's, as a member of the wealthy and powerful Elliott clan, she'd had some experience with photographers snapping unexpected pictures of her.

A guard with a walkie-talkie in his hand reached over and opened one of the passenger doors to the limo for them.

"In you go," Zeke said.

Once they were inside and the car was moving, she asked, "Where are we going?"

"The Waldorf-Astoria," he said. "I always stay there when I'm in town."

Oh. She just prayed she didn't run into an acquaintance of her grandparents or one of the other Elliotts. Dressed as she was and in the company of reputed bad-boy rocker Zeke Woodlow, she'd definitely raise some eyebrows.

As soon as the limo cleared the guard's security post and hit the street, flashbulbs started to go off— just as Zeke had predicted. Fortunately, the stoplight at the corner was green, so the limo was able to make a clean getaway before anyone could press a camera against the car window. Summer fervently hoped no one had gotten a photo of her.

The Waldorf-Astoria was a different matter. When they arrived at its front entrance, security guards and handlers got out first from a car that had preceded the limo to the hotel.

She was soon thankful for the extra protection. As she and Zeke alighted from their car and hurried to the front door of the hotel, several security guards held back photographers and squealing fans.

Summer kept her head down and tried to shield her face with the raised collar of her coat and with the hand that she kept cupped over her eyes. She didn't want to be too obvious about avoiding photographers because she didn't want to make Zeke suspicious. On the other hand, she didn't even want to think about the repercussions of their photo landing on Page Six of the *New York Post* in the morning.

Once they were inside, she followed Zeke as he made his way to the elevator bank.

He glanced down at her in amusement. "Camera shy?"

"Do they always know where you're staying?" she asked in exasperation.

He shrugged. "They always do. Of course, in New York, I'm always at the Waldorf, so there's not much guess work."

"And do the handlers never leave you?"

He tossed her a sly grin. "You're about to find out," he said as he stepped into the elevator behind her, punched a button and watched the doors slide shut.

In the confined space, she was again very aware of him—of his all-male aura and blatant sex appeal. "Where are we going?" she asked, trying to keep her tone even.

"My suite," he said as the doors to the elevator opened again.

Tell him. Tell him. It really was past time that she came clean about what she was doing here. They were about to go back to his hotel room!

And yet, the words wouldn't come. She was caught up in the strange excitement that seemed to exist between them.

They walked past another security guard—one

whose job evidently was to ensure that no uninvited guests made their way to Zeke's door—and then they were inside Zeke's suite.

Classical music wafted through the space. Following him down a long corridor, she stopped at the entrance to a huge parlor graced by a large chandelier. A dining room table large enough to sit twelve sat along one end of the room, while a fireplace and couches and chairs clustered at another.

The decor was tasteful and not at all tacky and lavish—the latter, she admitted, was sort of what she'd been expecting of a rock sensation's hotel accommodations.

"Now, you know why I always stay at the Waldorf," he said with a quick grin, dropping his jacket onto a nearby chair.

"Mmm," she said as he took her coat and bag from her.

She was used to understated luxury. She'd grown up surrounded by it. She just hadn't expected it from his quarter, but since he had no reason to assume she'd be anything but very impressed, she refrained from saying something committal.

He stood inches from her, and they stared at each other.

"If you'd like to use the bathroom to freshen up," he said, breaking the tension, "it's down the hall and to the right."

"Th-thanks."

Her voice sounded breathless to her own ears. She needed time to think, time to figure out what to do.

When she continued not to make a move, he stepped aside for her.

She felt heat rise to her face. "I—I'll be right back."

She cursed the fact that she kept stumbling over her words. Could she seem any more devoid of poise?

Behind her, she heard him say, "I'm going to change shirts."

"Sure." She tried to sound nonchalant, but she felt his every step behind her.

She stopped in the narrow hallway, before the open door to the bathroom, and turned back toward him, nearly colliding with him in the process.

He reached out to steady her, and they both froze, his hands on her upper arms.

His eyes, she noted again hazily, were the most incredible blue that she'd ever seen.

"I've wanted to do this," he said thickly.

"What?" she breathed.

"This." He bent his head and kissed her.

The kiss was electric, and she felt it clear down to her toes.

When he broke away, he said, "This is going to sound crazy, but I feel as if I know you. As if I knew you before tonight, I mean."

"Not crazy. I feel the same way," she confessed.

How could she explain? It *was* crazy. Yet, she felt as if she'd known him—had been waiting for this moment—her entire life.

He bent his head again, and she waited for the already familiar scent and flavor of him.

The kiss this time was a slow and erotic dance, and she found herself leaning back against the wall for support.

She shuddered as he took the kiss deeper, and she opened to him, sliding her hands up his chest and to his shoulders to draw him closer. Pressed against him, she felt every inch of his lean, muscular form, from his firm thighs to the hard plane of his chest.

His lips moved from hers to trail kisses along her jawline to the sensitive spot below her ear. When his lips traced the delicate shell of her ear, a moan escaped her.

She felt a stab of pure lust. She'd never had the teenage crushes that other girls had had on movie stars and celebrities. She'd been too sensible for that type of thing. Now, though, confronted by a real rock star, her resistance crumbled like a house of sand.

His hands ran down her sides, over her hips and then to her back, molding her to him.

"We have to stop," she murmured.

"Right," he said, intent on kissing her neck.

She turned her head to the side to give him better access. "This is wrong."

"But it feels so right."

She couldn't argue with that logic.

"I've been seeing you in my dreams," he said.

"Sounds lovely."

He laughed against her throat. "It has been." He raised his head and looked into her eyes. "But the real thing is better."

He cupped her face and delivered a searing kiss.

When he finally lifted his head, they were both breathing hard. "Trust me?"

She nodded.

He bent and, sliding an arm behind her knees, lifted her as if she weighed no more than a feather.

She pulled his head down for another scorching kiss, then he headed for the room at the end of the hall.

The everyday, sensible Summer Elliott would have panicked by now. *This* Summer Elliott, however, could only feel an overwhelming sense of anticipation.

Release your inner goddess…. Release your inner goddess….

Yes. It wasn't just that her clothes were different tonight. Her inhibitions had also evaporated faster than water in the desert.

Listening to Zeke sing one slow-burn love song

after another, then being in his presence—hearing that sexy voice, looking into his blue eyes, feeling his arousing touch—her defenses were at a low ebb.

He carried her into a room that was expensively decorated and set her down at the foot of a king-size bed.

His fingers went to the hem of her sweater. "You don't mind if I get rid of this, do you? I have this need to touch you."

The sensible Summer Elliott was alarmed, but the uninhibited Summer just said, "Please."

The top came off, and he tossed it aside, his eyes widening with appreciation as he took in her wine-colored demi bra.

"Beautiful," he muttered.

She shivered in response to his blatant appreciation. She was thankful now that she'd let Scarlet coax her into wearing her sexiest underwear—underwear that, not coincidentally, she'd been talked into buying by her sister on their most recent shopping trip together.

She'd thought she'd have little use for the satin bra and matching panties. In fact, she remembered arguing with Scarlet last night and saying, "I don't see why I need to wear sexy underwear to the concert. After all, it's not as if anyone is going to see it."

Scarlet had sighed impatiently. "It's all part of dressing the role. If you dress sexier, you'll feel and act sexier."

Now Zeke caressed her with his fingertips, tracing

circles on her shoulders before feathering downward over her arms and then the tops of her breasts.

If he'd been anything but gentle, she'd have turned and fled. Instead, she felt herself melting under his tenderness.

He lowered the strap of her bra and his hand came up to cup the exposed breast, the pad of his thumb flicking over the nipple and making it hard and distended. The look on his face was dark, intense and clouded with desire.

A low whimper escaped from her. Her knees felt like jelly, while all her most sensitive spots were charged with awareness. When he pulled her against him and took her nipple in his mouth, she sagged against him, running her fingers through his hair.

With one hand, he unhooked her bra and pulled it off. His mouth moved to her other breast, and his hands roamed, busy with divesting her of her skirt. Dimly, she heard her skirt rustle to the ground, even as she concentrated on the pleasurable sensations of his mouth at her breast.

When he finally pulled back, his gaze swept over her and widened. She was dressed only in her panties, thigh-high hose and long boots.

"Wow." Yanking his shirt over his head, he added jokingly, "Guess I'll have to level the playing field."

She drank him in as he undressed. He was gorgeous, his chest flat and muscled, his body lean and strong.

When they came together again, it was all questing hands and torrid kisses.

She felt his erection press against her, and rubbed against it.

He raised his head and groaned. "I want you."

"Yes."

"You're a fantasy come to life."

"I'll bet," she teased, looking down at herself. "Stiletto boots and hose?"

"Oh, yeah." His eyes glinted. "Sit back and I'll help you off with them."

Obediently, she sat on the bed behind her and raised her leg.

Slowly, his eyes never leaving hers, he lowered the zipper of one boot and tossed it aside. He rolled down her stocking, tossed it aside as well, and then pressed a hot kiss to the inside of her ankle.

She'd never been more aroused in her life. Mesmerized, she watched him do the same to her other leg.

Afterward, he kicked off his shoes and undid his jeans, pulling the latter off along with his underwear, so that he stood before her naked and aroused.

"You're gorgeous," she said.

He quirked a brow, amusement crossing his face. "Same to you." He glanced around, then walked over to a carry-on bag on a nearby chair. After some rustling, he pulled something out and turned back to the bed. "For a second, I thought I didn't have any."

She glanced at the small packet in his hand. Protection. Suddenly, the enormity of what she was about to do hit her, and she gulped. "I guess this is as good a moment as any to tell you—"

"Yes?"

"I've never done this before."

Three

Summer watched as Zeke stopped, looking stunned. "Never?"

She shook her head, uncertain of his reaction. "Never."

She could swear she heard him murmur, "I thought so."

"What?"

"Nothing." He looked bemused. "It looks like it's a set of firsts." He paused. "I've never gone to bed with a virgin."

"Oh." She digested that information for a second. "Not even in high school?"

"Nope." Then he teased, "Making some assumptions, aren't we?"

She felt herself blush with embarrassment.

He held her gaze. "We don't have to if you're not ready."

Here it was, she thought. Her last chance to back out. Strangely, though, she realized it was the last thing she wanted. "I still want to," she whispered. "I still want you."

He nodded, and his shoulders relaxed. "Believe me, you couldn't want me any more than I want you right now."

Turning, he walked to the adjacent bathroom.

"What are you doing?" she asked.

"Getting some lubrication," he said over his shoulder. "We're going to need it."

She sat up on the bed.

He came back, set a tube down on the night table and ripped open the foil packet that he'd retrieved earlier.

"Let me," she said, gazing at him. "Teach me."

He swallowed—hard.

"Please," she said, reaching out a hand.

He took her hand and guided her, letting her roll the protection onto him. His eyes closed with pleasure.

She continued to stroke him even with the protection on, and he showed her what to do.

"Ah," he breathed, opening his eyes, which were cloudy with desire. "I'm about to come out of my skin."

She held her arms out to him, and he came down beside her on the bed, gathering her into his embrace. He began to kiss her, starting with her lips, then moving to her neck and shoulders and lower.

She felt languorous, wanton and sexy, and one by one, her muscles relaxed. This was better than a Swedish massage, she thought, and they hadn't even reached climax yet.

He kneaded her flesh while his lips touched here and there, making her come alive.

She shifted restlessly under the gentle onslaught. Finally, when she thought she couldn't stand any more, he opened the tube on the night table, rubbed some gel between his fingers and started massaging her intimately.

"Oh, Zeke!"

"Shh," he said soothingly. "Just feel."

How could she just feel? Quivering, she grasped his upper arm. She felt like a bow that was being pulled tight and then tighter.

Distantly, she heard Zeke crooning to her, and then he was there beside her, gathering her close, as his fingers continued to work and she went over the edge, shaking with her release.

When she finally came down to earth, she turned heavy eyes toward him.

"Now I want you," she whispered.

"Glad to hear that." His gaze intent, he moved

over her, positioning himself between her thighs. He gave her a quick, hard kiss. "I'll try not to hurt you. Just concentrate on kissing me."

His hands and lips soothed as he continued his inexorable move forward.

She felt stretched and full. Fear intruded for a moment, but before she could dwell on it, he thrust forward, burying himself within her.

She pulled away from their kiss and gasped. The pain had been sharp but fleeting. A feeling of fullness remained, and beneath that, pleasure.

"Did I hurt you?" he asked, his face etched with concern.

"It's better now. The pain was over quickly."

He smiled. "But this isn't."

He started to move then and taught her how to move with him, setting up a slow rhythm, while he whispered encouragement in her ear and described how she made him feel.

She felt wound tight, and the tension only seemed to build as he whispered intimate questions in her ear and coaxed answers from her.

In another life, she'd have been red with embarrassment. But tonight, she felt loose and carefree.

He was incredible, and he was absolutely devastating her. He crooned some sexy lyrics in her ear, and she nearly came undone.

His pace quickened then, and his breathing

became labored and harsh. Just when she thought the coil within her was going to spring free, he thrust once, twice....

Her release came seconds before his powerful climax. He tensed, thrust, jerked, and then went slack against her.

When their breathing had slowed and their hearts had stopped racing, she said huskily, "You've got great timing."

He guffawed and kissed her on the nose. "I'll take that as a compliment." He moved to her side, slung an arm over her and snuggled her close.

Zeke woke up happy, but the emotion was fleeting.

Sunlight streamed into the room. He could tell because, though his eyes were closed, a bright orange haze played before his eyes.

His lips turned up.

He'd dreamed long and well. He'd imagined himself composing a song—the song that had been torturing him for months.

He hummed a few bars. It was the first time that he'd woken up and been able to hang on to any piece of the song.

He figured there was a reason that he'd finally had a breakthrough, and that reason was lying next to him. *She* was the primary reason that last night had been superb.

He moved his arm, reaching for her…and came up empty. Just to be sure, he moved his arm again experimentally, patting the mattress. Nothing.

He blinked and sat up. Looking around, his happy mood fled as he realized her clothes were gone. He didn't hear movement in the suite, either.

Still, on the off chance that he was wrong, he swung his legs off the bed and padded out of the room naked.

After checking the bathroom and then the living room area, he had to face facts: she'd left without so much as saying Goodbye, thanks for a great time. And, to make matters worse, he didn't even have her full name.

His stomach plunged. Damn it. He battled the urge to punch a wall until common sense kicked in. He could picture the headline in tomorrow's paper if he gave in to frustration: Bad-boy Rocker Trashes Hotel Suite.

Stalking back to the bedroom, he raked his hand through his hair. He needed time to think. He had to find her—she was the key to his creativity. But he couldn't go around broadcasting the fact that he'd just spent the night with a woman that he knew only as Caitlin.

His eyes landed on a telltale blood stain darkening the bed sheet, and he cursed. She'd seemed innocent, and she had been.

He had to find her. He felt as though he'd finally found what he'd been looking for, and now that he had, he wasn't about to let her slip through his fingers.

He glanced at the alarm clock on the night table. It was still early.

While he mulled over what to do, he ordered breakfast from room service, then padded into the bathroom to shower and then dress. He knew from experience that before long, Marty and umpteen other people would be calling him about the day ahead. The only reason he'd gotten a bit of a reprieve this morning was because last night had been his last benefit concert for Musicians for a Cure for the time being.

By the time room service arrived, he'd hit on only one possible plan—other than hiring a private investigator. He figured Caitlin had probably bought herself a concert ticket in advance—probably with a credit card—so someone at the box office should have a full name on file. If he could just get access to that information…

Sitting down, he dug into a breakfast of pancakes, scrambled eggs and bacon. Absently, he flicked through the local newspapers that he'd requested be delivered to him along with breakfast.

Taking a sip of his coffee, he turned to Page Six of the *New York Post* to see if there was any mention of last night's concert in the gossip columns…and nearly spewed his coffee.

As coffee sloshed over the rim of his cup, he shot out of his chair to avoid getting burned.

There, staring up at him, was a paparazzi shot of him and Caitlin ducking into an elevator at the Waldorf last night. The first line of the article read: "Heiress Scarlet Elliott and rocker Zeke Woodlow's midnight encounter!"

Heiress?

What the hell?

Anger rose like bile in his throat. Had he been taken for a ride last night?

But no, she'd apparently been a virgin. Still, his brows snapping together, he wondered whether she'd just been fulfilling some odd fantasy about a rock star, a hotel room and losing her virginity.

His eyes flicked over the rest of the article. Apparently Caitlin was, in actuality, Scarlet Elliott, member of the powerful Elliott clan and heiress to the Elliott publishing fortune. Even he'd heard of the family and Elliott Publication Holdings.

If he remembered correctly, the Elliotts owned everything from the highly regarded news periodical *Pulse* to the celebrity-watching magazine *Snap*.

Well, at least now he knew how to track down "Caitlin." Page Six had done his work for him. Unfortunately, he now had another problem on his hands: Caitlin wasn't just another rock groupie. She was an heiress—one whom he'd just deflowered—

and the two of them were splashed all over the morning paper!

He hoped to God that the fact that her family was in the publishing business was a mere coincidence and not the reason Caitlin—or Scarlet, or whatever the hell her name was—had tracked him down. Otherwise, there was going to be hell to pay, and if he was going to pay through the nose, he was going to make damn sure that his Daphne look-alike did, too.

Picking up the phone, he punched in the number for directory assistance and asked for the address for Elliott Publication Holdings.

Summer stared at the wall of her cubicle at EPH's headquarters.

She couldn't believe how her life had changed in twenty-four hours.

Since when had she become so impulsive? So stupid? She winced. And, what was she going to tell John?

Thankfully, John was still away on his business trip. After all, what could she say to him?

Oh, hi. I'm so glad you're back. Yes, yes…no, nothing much happened. I just lost my virginity to a rock star. I guess you've heard of him? Zeke Woodlow.

She groaned, leaned forward and rubbed her face with her hands again.

She felt ill, as if her stomach muscles would

remain clenched for the rest of her life. Hysteria was barely being held at bay.

What had possessed her?

In a word: Zeke.

The answer popped into her head unbidden, and she felt herself grow hot.

In fact, she couldn't remember anything about last night without feeling herself heat up. It had been one of the most wonderful experiences of her life. Despite Zeke's reputation in the press as a player who changed women as quickly and easily as he changed clothes, he'd been sweet and gentle and considerate. She couldn't imagine a better way to have lost her virginity.

Still, she'd lain in her bedroom last night and agonized till the sun had come up over what had made her act so recklessly. She hadn't had much to drink. Sure, there'd been a couple fortifying glasses of wine back at *Charisma*'s offices while Scarlet had helped her dress. But those drinks had been hours before she'd stepped foot inside the Waldorf, and she'd only had a beer with Zeke in his dressing room.

No, she couldn't blame the alcohol, as much as that would provide an easy out.

Of course, she'd also recently been witnessing her family come apart as a result of her grandfather's ridiculous challenge. Certainly, there'd been more tension around *The Buzz*.

But whom was she kidding? She was a lowly copy editor. If there was pressure to be felt, it rested squarely on the shoulders of her uncle Shane, who was editor in chief of *The Buzz*.

Thinking of work, she winced as she remembered dragging herself to the office this morning. She'd been an hour late. Shane had seen her come in and quirked an eyebrow.

If she'd been productive in the hour since she'd arrived, she'd have felt better. Unfortunately, she'd managed the sum total of turning on her computer, making three trips to the pantry for coffee, water and more coffee, and staring at her cubicle wall.

There was no avoiding the last possible explanation for her uncharacteristic behavior last night: John. In the few weeks since he'd proposed, she'd felt jittery and unable to shake the feeling that she was making a mistake. Instead of planning her wedding, she'd found herself avoiding the subject of her upcoming nuptials whenever Scarlet or her grandmother had brought it up.

But had she slept with Zeke *because of* or *despite* her engagement to John? Had she unconsciously been trying to sabotage her engagement, or had she just been unable to resist Zeke?

She still couldn't believe she'd lost her virginity so casually after hanging on to it for so long. The formerly, sensible Summer Elliott had convinced a reluctant John to wait until their wedding night. She'd envisioned her wedding as the culmination of the careful screening process that she'd begun after college, winnowing down a small field of men to find The One. What more appropriate time to lose her virginity than on her wedding night?

It hadn't seemed like much of a hardship to wait. She'd known that if she kept to her five-year plan, she would be married by twenty-six. And, she'd reasoned, if pop star Jessica Simpson could resist the delectable Nick Lachey until their wedding night, she could certainly resist John.

Then, last night, she'd fallen into bed with Zeke after knowing him mere hours. Even more damning, she hadn't thought about John. Not once. Not until this morning.

She was whatever they called the female version of a cad. A fiend. Slime. She was only surprised that she hadn't grown scales and recoiled with horror when she'd faced the mirror this morning.

She sighed.

Whenever something had bothered her in the past, she'd always turned to Scarlet. This morning, she'd snuck back into the townhouse when it was still dark and had slept in, mumbling, when Scarlet had checked on her before leaving for work, that she wasn't feeling well.

She'd intended to keep last night to herself, to

bring it to her grave, if possible, or at least to avoid disclosing the facts as long as possible. But since her brain waves were on automatic pilot straight to Zeke, she figured she couldn't hold out against a teary confession to Scarlet much longer.

She got up. In fact, another two minutes was about as long as she could hold out.

When she got to the *Charisma* offices on the floor below, she walked toward Scarlet's cubicle until she heard her sister's voice coming from a nearby meeting room.

Bad timing, she thought. Scarlet was obviously in the middle of a conversation with someone else.

When she reached the open doorway to the meeting room, she saw her sister standing behind a conference table laden with photos and magazine clippings.

Scarlet's eyes widened as they connected with hers. Her sister made a quick, seemingly surreptitious, shooing motion with one hand.

Before she could digest the meaning, however, she took a step forward, and the man standing in front of the conference table turned around.

Her eyes collided with the impossibly blue, impossibly angry gaze of Zeke Woodlow.

Four

Zeke stared at the woman in the doorway. His eyes told him what his gut had already figured out: The woman behind the conference table was not the woman with whom he'd had a torrid night of mind-blowing sex. The woman in front of him was.

It all made sense now. Identical twins. Of course.

When he'd stepped into the conference room minutes before, he hadn't been able to shake the feeling that he'd tracked down the wrong person, despite her resemblance to the woman of last night. He just hadn't experienced that same kick-in-the-gut feeling of awareness…of being attuned to her.

But just what kind of game had these two been playing with him? The small part of his mind not given over to simmering anger took note of the fact that the woman he'd spent the night with was dressed much more like he'd imagined her. He hadn't been wrong last night when he'd thought that her clothes didn't suit her. She really was all cashmere and pearls.

His gaze raked her from head to foot before his eyes narrowed on the diamond ring on her finger.

Hell. She was engaged? What other surprises did she have in store for him?

Because she continued to stare at him, frozen in place, he glanced back at the woman behind the table, who'd done a good job of holding him off and attempting to cover for her sister. "Scarlet Elliott, right?" he sneered, before swinging back to the woman whom he'd last seen sprawled naked across his sheets. "And you're her identical twin…?"

"Summer," she supplied in a barely audible tone.

"Well, Summer," he said with false pleasantness, "there's no need to look horrified. I have to ask, though, how often have you and Scarlet played this identity-switching game? I'm finding it hard to believe I'm your first victim."

"How did you find me?" she blurted.

"Now, that's a good question, isn't it?" he asked in the same pleasant tone. He held out a copy of the

New York Post, folded and turned to Page Six. "Let's just say I got some unexpected help."

She took the newspaper from him and scanned it, her eyes widening.

"Yeah. Exactly." He glanced at Scarlet, then back at Summer. "Your sister tried to cover for you, but she's not that good an actress."

Scarlet bristled. "Look, Zeke, insult me all you want, but I resent having you take cheap shots at my sister. You may think, just because you're the current it-boy of the music world, that you can come in here and start flinging accusations, but I can have you thrown out so fast it'll make that rock-star hair of yours look more than artfully disheveled."

He raised his eyebrows. "Well, well, a debutante who doesn't bother with the kid-glove treatment. I guess that was your spandex-and-cleavage outfit that Summer was wearing last night?"

Summer took a step forward. "Stop it, both of you." She turned to him. "We need to talk."

"Yeah, we're in agreement on that at least. You owe me some answers."

"Not here, though," she said quickly. "There's another conference room upstairs, near my desk, that's rarely used. We can talk there privately."

As he turned to follow Summer out of the office, Scarlet threw him a warning look that blared: *Watch it. I can still have you thrown out of here on your ear.*

He gave her a parting grin that was full of insouciance.

As he followed Summer down the brightly patterned hall to the elevator bank, he noted that, if anything, she looked even sexier this morning than she had last night.

She was dressed in kitten heels, pearls and a twin sweater set. The retro look was demure, yet alluring. While last night's outfit had been like a green flag at a professional car race, this was more stop than go, and sexier as a result.

Realizing the direction that his mind was heading in, he put the brakes on his thoughts. Annoyed, he reflected that, while he had every reason to be mad as hell at her, he was still attracted to her.

When they got to the floor above, he noticed the decorating scheme changed from turquoise blue and edgy to red with lots of glass and chrome. He figured they were in the offices of another magazine in the EPH publishing empire.

As if reading his mind, she turned and said over her shoulder, "This floor houses *The Buzz.*"

"Let me guess," he said dryly. "You work for *The Buzz.*" He reined in his temper once again at the thought that he'd been taken in by some reporter's scheme to get access. Marty would have a fit.

"Yes," she acknowledged, then added, "Did anyone recognize you when you came in?"

"I'm surprised you didn't hear the squeals and screams up on the eighteenth floor."

She stared at him in astonishment.

"Worried?" he asked, unable to resist toying with her. Only after a deliberate pause did he explain, "This is New York City. Of course, anyone who recognized me was too blasé to care. That's why celebrities love New York."

When they got to the conference room, she shut the door behind them, and he sat on the edge of the conference table and folded his arms.

"Now, where were we?" he asked with outward pleasantness. He raised a hand as if to stop her reply. "Oh, yeah, you were about to explain how you forgot to mention you're a reporter, why you snuck out of my hotel room in the middle of the night and why you happened to be dressed like Scarlet." He added, focusing at the diamond ring on her finger, "Not to mention the fact that you've got a fiancé hidden away somewhere."

"He isn't hidden away. He's on a business trip."

"Even better." He felt a stab of jealousy. "I wonder how the future Mr. Summer Elliott will feel knowing his fiancée lost her virginity in a hotel room to a man she'd known only a few hours."

She flushed.

He cocked his head. "A little extreme, don't you think? Losing your virginity for the sake of a reporting assignment? Or was this just some prank that you and your sister concocted—sort of the last hurrah before the wedding?"

"Stop it! It's not the way you're making it seem."

"'Stop it,'" he mimicked. "Is that the best that you can do? Come on, Summer, let go of the uptown girl. Let's hear you really swear."

He was furious with her and even more furious with himself. He, who had a reputation for bad-boy ways and a sullen sulk, had been used and abused by Ms. Prim and Proper. The newspapers would have a field day.

"I don't need to swear," she snapped back. "And you're one to talk. Do you jump into bed with a different groupie every night?"

"Jealous?"

"That's ridiculous."

He decided not to enlighten her about his promiscuity or lack thereof. He wasn't a monk by any stretch of the imagination, but the news reports about him were usually overblown.

Besides, what could he say to explain jumping into bed with her last night? Whenever I see you, I hear a symphony? How corny was that? Not to mention that The Supremes had made it a hit song long ago. Yet, it was close to the truth. If only he could get that damn song down on paper…

Aloud, he countered, "You lied to me. Twice. First

not telling me you're an heiress, now this." He gestured at her hand. "You're engaged."

"I didn't lie."

He chuckled cynically. "Really, *Caitlin?*"

"That's my middle name. Summer Caitlin Elliott."

"And do you usually go by your middle name?"

Her shoulders lowered. "No, but I was only trying to buy a little time—"

"A little time till when?" he interrupted. "Until we were in bed together? Until the newspapers picked up the story?"

She threw up her hands. "Okay! You're right, I'm wrong! Is that what you want to hear?" She blew out a breath. "If you'd just let me explain."

"So explain."

She squared her shoulders. "I'm just a copy editor here, but my goal has been to become a reporter. Everyone knows you're the hottest thing in the music world right now. You're always getting mentioned in *The Buzz* and in other entertainment magazines. I thought that if I could convince you to do an interview…except I knew that you rarely granted interviews—"

"That's because I prefer to let my music speak for me."

So, he'd been right. She had been after an interview. *Screwed for an interview.* He shook his head. *Great.* There was a song in that, he could feel it.

She twisted her hands together. "I know it all sounds bad."

He quirked a brow. "Honey, it doesn't only sound bad. It *is* bad."

He'd begun to calm down, but being alone in the same room with her had his body humming. There were also things that still didn't make sense to him. For starters, she'd been a virgin. Now that he'd started to think logically about all that had happened and all that he'd found out so far, that piece of the puzzle just didn't fit. Unless, of course, she'd been swept away by lust, too.

Keeping his voice even, he said, "You still haven't explained how dressing like Scarlet figures into the picture."

She sighed. "I tried to approach you after the benefit concert on Wednesday night, but I couldn't get by security. Scarlet suggested I'd have better luck if I pretended to be a groupie." She paused. "Of course, I left my engagement ring at home."

He had one other question. "And sleeping with me?"

She flushed. "That wasn't part of the plan. It— I— It just happened."

Not the satisfaction that he was looking for, he thought, but it was something. He had every reason to be furious at her for misleading him and not revealing she was engaged. Yet, there was something about her that soothed his soul even as it inflamed his lust.

Besides, he figured her engagement couldn't be much of an obstacle if she'd been a virgin until last night. And, then there was the matter of *the* song. With that thought, an idea started to take hold.

She blinked rapidly. "I owe you a big apology. I never meant to mislead you. I was waiting for the right moment last night to tell you why I was there, but that moment never came." She drew a quivering breath. "I'm sorry."

He looked down for a moment, then back up at her. "What if I said I'll agree to do the interview?"

Her eyes widened. "You will? B-but why?"

His lips teased upward. "Maybe I've never had someone go to so much trouble just to get within speaking distance of me." *Or, for the matter,* he added silently, *into my bed.*

She looked uncertain for a moment.

"Well?" he said. "How about it?"

"We slept together!"

He shrugged and made sure to keep his voice neutral. "So? That's in the past—" albeit, the very recent past "—and it's not as if we have an ongoing relationship. Besides, this is the entertainment business, not global geopolitics. No one hesitates to use every connection, no matter how it comes about. And anyway, the press thinks I was out with Scarlet last night, not you."

She looked down, contemplating what he'd said, and he found himself holding his breath.

In the morning light shafting through the room's windows, she looked delectable, and he felt like the Big Bad Wolf. Last night hadn't sated his hunger for her. Not by a long shot.

Finally, she looked up at him with those amazing pale-green eyes. "Okay," she said, then added, "Thank you."

He let go of the breath he was holding. The seduction of Summer Elliott had begun, only she didn't know it yet.

"You slept with him?" Scarlet's mouth gaped open.

"A little louder," Summer said dryly. "The next table over hasn't heard you."

They were sitting in a booth in the employees' cafeteria on the fourth floor of EPH, where she and Scarlet regularly had lunch together. The cafeteria was a quicker and easier choice than beating the throngs that clogged the Manhattan streets downstairs at lunchtime.

"Didn't you tell him that you were there as a reporter?" Scarlet persisted.

"Er, we didn't quite get to that part."

"You didn't get to that part?"

Under other circumstances, Summer would have thought this scene was funny. For the second time today, she had managed to flabbergast someone: at the

moment Scarlet, whom she knew to be usually unflap-
pable, and earlier Zeke, who certainly appeared that
way. Since she was a play-by-the-rules girl, this was
a day of firsts for her. Aloud, she said, "Haven't you
ever slept with a guy on a first date?"

"Never."

"Never?"

Scarlet shook her head.

Apparently, for once, she'd outdone her twin in
outrageousness. She didn't know whether to laugh or
cry, which was another sign, she supposed, that she
was verging on hysteria.

"Anyway," Scarlet persisted, the salad in front of
her forgotten, "this isn't about me and this isn't just
about sleeping with a guy. This is about losing your
virginity to some bad-boy rock star that you barely
know when you said for years that you'd wait for
your wedding night."

Summer knew that Scarlet had neither completely
understood nor shared her vow of celibacy, but her
sister had respected it. Now maybe even respect had
flown out the window.

Summer winced at the thought, before joking
weakly, "Thanks. Could you maybe make it sound
more sordid and trashy?"

"And what about John?" Scarlet demanded, then
shook her head. "I don't get it. Why lose your virginity now, when the wedding night is around the corner?"

Summer had been dwelling on the same question since leaving Zeke's hotel room.

After the confrontation with Zeke at the office that morning, she'd resigned herself to getting no work done and had popped outside and sat in a café, sipping tea, until lunchtime.

She'd had plenty of time to think, and to dwell on the fact that she'd never before experienced the same restless, I've-got-to-have-you-now attraction that she had last night with Zeke. The attraction defied explanation and logic—he was unlike her in many ways, and definitely didn't fit her normal taste in men—but there it was.

She'd also started to think that maybe her relationship with John was sexless because it was passionless. There was just no spark. Oh, she loved him, and he'd said he loved her, but maybe they'd both mistaken convenience and warm affection for sexual love.

She felt comfortable and safe with John and she understood him…but maybe that wasn't enough.

"What are you thinking?" Scarlet asked.

"I've been asking myself about John all morning."

"Yes?"

Summer shrugged resignedly, pushing her salad aside. She wasn't going to eat another bite. "I don't know. Maybe I wanted so badly to stick to my five-year plan and settle down that I ignored doubts I was having about my relationship with John."

And maybe she *was* crazy. After all, she was basing conclusions on one night of passion. Passion seemed like such an unreliable emotion compared to the solid and stable relationship that she had with John. Or rather, she amended, the solid and stable relationship that she'd *thought* she had with John.

"What are you going to tell him?" Scarlet asked.

"I don't know," she admitted. "He's still out of town, but I'll eventually have to tell him what happened." She smiled wryly. "However, the fact that the newspapers think it was you last night has bought me some time. Otherwise, I'd be afraid that John would have heard the gossip somehow even though he's out of town. This way, I get to break the news to him gently when he gets back."

She gave Scarlet an apologetic look. "Sorry for getting you mixed up in this."

"Don't worry about it. My reputation can use the spark right now," Scarlet said with dry humor.

A cell phone rang, and Summer realized it was hers. She dug it out of her purse and shrank as she noticed it was John calling.

"It's John," she said to Scarlet before pressing the Talk button and saying brightly, "Hi."

"Hey, yourself," John's deep voice sounded from the phone. "I've missed you."

What could she say to that? "How's your trip?"

"Great," he said, his voice reflecting his good

mood. "We got the deal wrapped up early, so guess what? I'll be flying back from Chicago this afternoon. In fact, I'm at the airport now."

Summer's stomach plummeted.

"How about catching dinner with me tonight?" John asked. "What about One If by Land, Two If by Sea?"

"Sure," she said weakly. One If by Land, Two If by Sea was reputed to be one of New York City's most romantic restaurants. It occupied a landmark eighteenth-century carriage house once owned by Aaron Burr.

"We're about to board," John said, breaking into her thoughts. "Can't wait to see you. Bye."

"Bye," she said before ending the call.

"Well?" Scarlet asked.

Summer looked at her, the weight of doom settling on her shoulders. "He's flying back early, and we're having dinner tonight."

Scarlet raised her water glass in a mock salute. "Showtime."

Five

John was waiting for her at the bar at One If by Land, Two If by Sea when Summer got there at six. She'd suggested an early dinner because she knew he'd be tired from his trip and, more importantly, she could meet him directly after work and thus circumvent having him pick her up at the townhouse. She wanted to avoid being alone with him tonight, given the news that she had to impart.

He slid off a bar stool. "Hey, sweetie."

She tried not to wince at the endearment. It reminded her that she was lower than a worm, that John had always treated her like a princess and that he didn't deserve what she was about to tell him.

When he leaned in for a quick peck on the lips, she looked away at the last moment so that his lips met her cheek.

She could see the slight puzzlement on his face as he pulled away.

"Is our table ready?" she asked cheerfully.

"I think so," he said.

He nodded to the bartender and settled his tab, then, with his hand at the small of her back, he guided her forward. A hostess showed them to their table, and John waited until Summer herself was seated before taking his own seat.

Settled in, he reached over and took her hand, rubbing the back of it in a circular motion with his thumb. "I missed you."

Summer smiled feebly.

What was wrong with her? Looking into John's caring dark brown eyes and catching sight of his disarming dimples, she questioned her decision and wondered whether she was about to compound one error with another. John was a man that any woman would be proud to be seen with. He was good-looking, hard-working, ambitious and reliable. In short, a catch in any sense of the word.

"I'm glad you're back," she responded, sliding her hand away. "Are you going to order some wine?"

He frowned. "Yes. I just hadn't gotten around to it yet." Nevertheless, he picked up the wine list and started reading it.

Summer took the opportunity to study him. The light from the overhead chandeliers caused his light brown hair to glint and gleam. He should have been perfect for her, but something had been missing.

Doubts. She'd been having them all along where John was concerned. Niggling doubts that hadn't gone away. But why, *why,* did she have to sleep with another man before she was willing to face them?

After the wine arrived, they ordered, then discussed John's trip. Because John traveled often for his high-octane career in advertising, he was often full of interesting stories about shooting TV commercials and developing promotional campaigns for new products.

"So, we sewed up the deal," he said, cutting into his beef Wellington. "Three print ads for watches by one of Hollywood's hottest actresses."

"I'm surprised she agreed to do it," Summer commented.

"So am I. A lot of film stars are reluctant to do ads in the United States because they're afraid it'll detract from their image. They'll do ads abroad, but only with the stipulation that those ads won't run in the U.S."

"So why do you think she agreed to do it?"

"Money," John replied. "This advertising campaign is going to cost our client a bundle, but the CEO thinks it's worth it because their target audience is the eighteen-to-twenty-four age group."

Summer had grown used to John throwing out advertising jargon as if it was second nature. He talked in terms of *target audiences, market share* and *campaigns.* She knew that being immersed in his career was part of what made John so successful at what he did.

As a waiter moved away with their plates, John said, "By the way, I saw that Scarlet was linked to Zeke Woodlow in today's gossip columns. Maybe she can convince him to do some ads."

Wine sloshed from the glass that Summer was raising to her lips. She watched as the spilled liquid caused a couple of angry red spots to spread on the formerly pristine tablecloth.

"Careful," John said.

She set down her glass with a thump and cleared her throat. She'd been waiting for the right moment to broach the subject of Zeke and now she was out of excuses. Dinner was over, and there was no time like the present.

"John, we have to talk," she blurted, waving off a waiter who had approached with dessert menus.

John looked at her inquiringly for an instant, then asked the waiter for the check. As the waiter moved off, he said, "So talk. You've seemed jumpy and distracted all night. I was wondering what was bothering you."

"This is hard," she began. Explain first and confess later, or confess first and explain later? She waffled.

"Yes?" he prompted.

"Something unexpected happened while you were away, and I—I came to some realizations."

He said nothing, just looked at her expectantly.

Tears threatened. She felt as if she were about to kick a puppy. Looking down, she said in a rush, "John, I can't marry you."

"What?" he said on a forced and skeptical laugh.

"It's not a joke."

"Why? I thought—"

She didn't let him finish. "I had sex with someone last night. Zeke Woodlow."

There it was. The harsh, glaring truth.

John looked as if she'd slapped him or thrown a bucket of ice water over his head.

"What did you say?"

"I slept with Zeke Woodlow last night. The gossip columns got it wrong. It wasn't Scarlet with Zeke. It was me." She took a deep breath, her eyes pleading with him for some understanding even though she neither deserved nor expected any. "I didn't plan it. I went to a Musicians for a Cure concert to try to land an interview with Zeke for *The Buzz*." She trailed off helplessly, "I don't know what happened…."

John snorted derisively. "Come on, Summer, you know what happened." His brows snapped together. "So you're now on a first-name basis with Zeke, are you?"

Realizing her mistake, Summer shook her head. "I don't blame you for being angry and hurt."

"Really?" he said sarcastically, then raked his fingers through his hair. "I go away for a few days and you sleep with someone else. Do you know how that makes me feel? You told me you wanted to wait for marriage."

"I know," she said guiltily, "and I've spent the past twenty-four hours wondering how and why last night happened. I wasn't drunk or too stressed out, but I realized I'd been pushing aside doubts about us."

"What doubts? We're perfect for each other. We want the same things out of life."

"Yes," she agreed, knowing she had to tread carefully, "but we lack spark. Maybe...maybe that's why it was so easy for us to put off sex for so long."

He said nothing.

"Maybe we love one another without being passionate about each other." She added softly, "You deserve to have some passion in your life, John. We both do."

John downed the rest of his wine in one swallow. "I could've been as passionate as any rock star, Summer, if you'd just given me the opportunity. Instead, I agreed to *your* terms about waiting until the wedding night."

She looked down, unable to hold his gaze. Catching sight of the engagement ring still sparkling on her finger, she tugged it off. Taking hold of his hand, she placed her ring in his palm and gently wrapped his fingers around it.

He stared down at their hands.

When the waiter came back to their table with the check, she reached for it, but John was faster.

Pulling his hand from hers, he said bitterly, "Allow me to pay for the last hurrah."

"You broke up with John," Scarlet repeated in disbelief.

Summer nodded. They were sitting in a bar near EPH, Summer having phoned Scarlet to meet her after her dinner with John.

"Why? Are you crazy?" Scarlet asked. "Why throw away a perfectly good relationship? So you slept with Zeke! So you made a mistake! That doesn't mean you should just throw away the man you love—the man you're going to marry. Everyone makes mistakes."

Summer shook her head. "You don't understand."

"Isn't John worth fighting for? If he can forgive you because he loves you, you two can put this behind you and move on with the life that you always intended to have together."

"It's not that simple. I'm not calling off the engagement because I slept with Zeke. I'm calling it off because sleeping with Zeke made me confront the doubts I'd been having about marrying John."

"Such as?"

"Maybe John and I love each other, but not in the sexual way that two people getting married should. Maybe it was easy for our relationship to remain sexless because it was passionless."

"Aren't you getting it backward?" her sister argued. "Maybe it was passionless because it was sexless."

"That's what I thought, but after last night I started to realize it was the other way." She paused. "John is a wonderful guy, but we just don't share that much passion."

Scarlet looked surprised, started to say something, and then stopped. Covering Summer's hand with her own, she said, "Are you sure you're not letting yourself be swayed by a night of great sex? Having sex for the first time can be heady stuff. It can screw up your thinking. You know, *Charisma* just ran a survey, and you wouldn't believe how many women, even today, feel they have to stick with the first man they sleep with."

"No," she said stubbornly, "it's not that, and I'm not confused. I have no intention of getting involved with Zeke just because I slept with him." *Just because I lost my virginity to him,* she added silently. She had no intention of compounding last night's mistake. "But if I'm sure of anything right now, it's that continuing to stay engaged to John would be wrong. I need time to sort things out."

"Are you sure this isn't just a case of cold feet?" Scarlet persisted.

"What?" she countered. "Cold feet from the day I got engaged? Months before the actual wedding?"

Scarlet sighed. "I guess you won't be the first woman to call off an engagement because she's realized it's a mistake."

Ironically, she found herself wanting to comfort Scarlet. She gave her sister a reassuring hug. "Cheer up! I finally let myself admit that John was so much like what I thought I wanted in a husband that I'd been ignoring the fact that I wasn't in love with him. At least the realization didn't strike at the altar."

"I guess I should be glad it didn't take that long," Scarlet murmured.

"What?" Summer asked.

"I said, I guess *he* should be glad it didn't take that long."

Summer nodded uncertainly. For a second, she'd thought Scarlet had responded with something completely different. Aloud, she said, "It's for the best, Scar. I'm sure of it. You'll see."

Zeke prowled around his hotel suite, half listening to his manager. It was almost nine o'clock on Friday night and within half an hour he'd be heading out to one of New York's hottest clubs, the celebrity hangout Lotus.

Like many celebrities, he was welcome with open arms at Manhattan's hot spots. Club owners were only too eager to toss free drinks and food at a star in exchange for free publicity, namely, having their club's name linked in the press with that of an A-list celeb.

Unfortunately, Marty had decided to stop by minutes ago from his own hotel room elsewhere in the building—ostensibly to discuss last night's benefit concert, but Zeke wasn't fooled.

Marty was a forty-something, balding music-industry veteran who'd been lucky enough and savvy enough to manage more than one great act during his career. But while his experience often made him invaluable, it also meant he could sniff potential trouble a mile away.

"So, you and Scarlet Elliott," Marty said, shaking his head. "I didn't even know you'd met."

"We didn't until this morning."

Marty frowned. "Come again? There was a photo—"

"I know about the damn photo," Zeke said irritably. "The reporter got it wrong. That was Summer Elliott last night." He added by way of explanation, "Scarlet's identical twin."

Zeke was still digesting everything that had occurred in the last twenty-four hours. *Damn it, she was engaged!*

"Elliott? As in Elliott Publication Holdings?" Marty asked.

"The one and same." Another piece of information, Zeke reflected, that she'd conveniently left out about herself. Hell, she'd known he'd assume she was some groupie.

Marty threw him a penetrating look. "Heiresses aren't your usual type. The publicist that we just hired for you has already been busy fielding questions from the media."

Zeke stopped in front of Marty. "What's he saying?"

Marty shrugged. "The usual. Fudging and leading the reporters on. You know, a half-hearted denial that you're involved with her, or rather, with the sister."

Zeke nodded. His public image was carefully cultivated. There was always a delicate dance with the media for maximum positive exposure and spin. Usually that meant leaving the public guessing about his love life, and appearing single and available and never too serious about any one woman for too long. Successive relationships helped keep his place as front-page news, and that suited him just fine. He knew he wasn't husband material, especially with a lifestyle that kept him on the road.

"So what's the truth?" Marty asked with his typical bluntness.

Zeke raked his fingers through his hair. "The truth is that she was a reporter after an interview with me."

He was not going to provide the intimate details about what had happened last night.

"I take it that you didn't give her the interview."

"That's right—"

Marty looked relieved.

"—but I've agreed to do an interview with her this week."

"What?" Mart stood up straighter. "I thought we'd been over this. All interview requests get vetted by me and the publicist. We want to make sure you're appearing in the right markets—"

"She works for *The Buzz.*"

"—and that the reporter knows the ground rules beforehand about what topics are off-limits—"

"Give me a break, Marty. This is going to be a short interview, not an in-depth profile for *Rolling Stone.*"

"It's not like you to cave in so easily to a request for an interview," Marty said, frowning.

Zeke shrugged. "This is going to sound nuts, but whenever I'm near her, I start hearing the song that's been playing in my head for the last few months and that I haven't been able to write. The only other thing that's been able to call it forth is a photograph that I have hanging back in the mansion in Los Angeles."

"She's your muse?" Marty asked, looking floored.

"Yeah, I guess you could say that."

Zeke watched his manager's face settle into unhappy lines. "Look, Zeke, I know you're into this songwriting stuff, but you're the hottest thing on the music scene right now. There are plenty of people who would love to be in your shoes, but they don't have your voice and they sure as hell don't have your sex appeal. Why mess with a good thing?"

They'd had this discussion half a dozen times. "Fame's fleeting, Mart."

"So? You can concentrate on the songwriting career later. For now, do yourself a favor and focus on putting out CDs and on touring to keep your name out there."

"I'm still mulling over that offer to write for a Broadway show."

Marty rolled his eyes. "Next thing you'll be telling me that you're getting serious about this Elliott chick. Remember, you've got an image as a heartthrob to maintain."

Zeke laughed and clapped him on the shoulder. "Marty, man, you're a damn pain in the rear."

Six

Emerging from the car, Summer looked up at The Tides and squared her shoulders. She felt as if she were twelve years old again and going in for a lecture from Gram and Granddad that was sure to end with her getting grounded.

Still, The Tides was home, and whenever she was stressed, she particularly welcomed its warm embrace. Probably not many people would think of the nearly 8,000-square-foot century-old mansion made of rusty sandstone as warm and inviting, but it was to her.

She breathed in the brisk sea air. Located in the Hamptons—an exclusive vacation community several hours east of New York City—the five-acre Elliott estate sat on a bluff overlooking the Atlantic Ocean.

Ever since her parents had died in a plane crash when she and Scarlet were only ten, she and her sister had been raised by Gram and Granddad at The Tides. Even now, she and Scarlet spent most weekends there.

Except, this morning Scarlet had begged off going out to The Tides, mumbling that she had things to do in the city. And when she'd tried to ask her sister where she'd gone last night—because Scarlet hadn't been home when Summer herself had finally gotten back to the townhouse after staying on at the bar with some coworkers after her sister's departure—Scarlet had clammed up.

She hoped Scarlet wasn't mad at her for breaking up with John in the way that she had. Her sister had seemed understanding enough yesterday, but this morning she'd been cool, abrupt and aloof, refusing to say where she'd been or with whom. They'd never kept secrets from each other in the past, so Scarlet's behavior had hurt.

Summer waved to Benjamin Trent, her grandparents' long-time groundskeeper, then climbed the steps to the front door.

Home. She put down her bag and tossed her jacket onto a nearby chair, looking around the house as she did so and taking in for the thousandth time the understated and elegant decor that was a testament to Gram's fine taste.

Footsteps sounded on the marble floor and a few seconds later, Gram emerged from the living room at the back of the house.

"Summer! What a lovely surprise!" Gram said, her voice colored by an Irish accent. "I wasn't sure if you were coming this weekend, with the wedding planning and all."

Wedding. She was reminded again of the conversation that lay ahead. Nevertheless, she smiled, then kissed her grandmother on the cheek. "Hello, Gram."

Her grandmother had been a nineteen-year-old seamstress in Ireland when Patrick Elliott had swept her off her feet. Now, though she was seventy-five, one could still detect some freckles on her pale skin and some auburn in the white hair that she always wore in an updo. Despite her somewhat frail health, she radiated warmth and cheer.

When Summer pulled back, she noticed Gram's eyes went to the door, then back to her.

"You're just in time for lunch. Scarlet hasn't joined you?"

"No, she said she had things to do in the city this weekend." She linked her arm with Gram's, and they started toward the breakfast room at the back of the house. "We'll have a lovely lunch anyway, won't we?"

"With you here, of course!"

She'd always felt protective toward Gram. Not only had Gram lost her son Stephen and his wife—Summer's parents—in a plane crash, but she'd also lost her seven-year-old daughter Anna to cancer. Adding to the strain, Granddad hadn't always been on the best of terms with his and Gram's surviving adult children.

When they got to the breakfast room, Olive—Benjamin's wife and the housekeeper at The Tides—greeted them warmly, and Gram asked her to set another place at the table.

Noticing that only three places were to be set, Summer asked, "Aren't Aunt Karen and Uncle Michael here?"

"Michael had to get back to the office yesterday to deal with pressing business and won't be back till this evening," Gram responded as they took their seats. "And Karen is resting." Gram's face clouded. "She's too tired to come down and will take her meal in her room later on."

"How is she doing?" Summer asked quietly. Her aunt, her uncle Michael's wife, had recently been diagnosed with breast cancer and had undergone a double mastectomy.

"Karen is never one to complain. I'm thankful the cancer hasn't spread, but the chemotherapy that she's taking as a precaution is going to take its toll."

Summer knew her cousins were concerned about

their mother, whose diagnosis remained guarded. The only bright light, Summer reflected, was that her cousin Gannon had just gotten married, and his younger brother, Tag, had recently gotten engaged to a wonderful woman. The celebrations had given her aunt something to look forward to.

Of course, Summer's own wedding, or nonwedding, was a different story.

She nearly jumped when her grandfather entered the room.

"Well," Patrick Elliott said in his usual booming voice, "if it isn't the return of the vagabond grandchild."

Unlike his wife, her grandfather showed gruff affection at best, but Summer was well used to it. She rose from her seat and kissed him on the cheek. "Granddad, you know I was here just last weekend." Settling back into her chair, she added, "It's just me this time, though. Scarlet decided to stay in the city."

Patrick Elliott took his seat as Olive, humming, came in with their bowls of chicken soup. "So how's your vagabond sister?"

Summer let out a half laugh.

"Patrick, you're incorrigible," Maeve said. "Stop teasing the poor girl."

Patrick's only response was a slight movement of his bushy eyebrows as he raised a spoonful of soup to his lips. Summer knew that if there was one person who could bring her grandfather to heel, it was Gram. He adored her.

Over lunch, they talked about current events and Maeve's charity work, as well as happenings in and around the Hamptons.

Just when Summer was starting to relax, however, and they were finishing up lunch over fresh berries and cream, Patrick nodded at her hand and said, "What happened to your sparkler?"

Darn. Leave it to her grandfather to zero in on her ringless hand. He'd probably noticed as soon as he'd come in and sat down, but, in typical Patrick Elliott fashion, he'd let his victim relax before going in for the kill.

Gulp. "I've called off the engagement."

"Have you now?" her grandfather asked pleasantly, as if they were discussing the weather.

"Oh, Summer," Maeve said. "Why?"

The million-dollar question, she thought. She wished she had a good answer. She knew that saying she'd lost her virginity to a globe-trotting musician whom she barely knew wouldn't play well with her Irish-Catholic grandparents.

"Um—" She cleared her throat. "I realized John and I just weren't suited for each other."

Maeve's brow furrowed. "But he seemed like such a nice man, and you two were like two peas in a pod."

"I think that was part of the problem," she said.

"We had no spark. We were too alike." Good grief, this was an awkward conversation to be having with her grandparents.

Patrick removed his napkin from his lap and set it down next to his plate, shaking his head. "Too alike? In my day, you met a fella with a steady job, you got married. You didn't worry that being responsible adults made you too alike."

Summer groaned inwardly.

"Patrick, do be quiet." Maeve patted her hand. "It's all right, dear."

Patrick stood. "I need to get back to work—like a responsible adult."

Watching her grandfather's retreating back, Summer said, "I guess I was speaking a foreign language to him."

Maeve sighed. "He'll get over it."

"I know he liked John." She looked at her grandmother. "They're similar in many ways. Smart, ambitious, hard-working." She hoped her grandfather didn't think her rejection of John amounted to a rejection of his values as well.

"He just wants to see you happy," Maeve said, "and he understands John." She added, her eyes twinkling, "After all, your grandfather's been a devoted husband for fifty-seven years. Naturally he's an expert on the formula for marital bliss."

"Naturally," Summer concurred.

Then they shared a laugh.

Thank God for her grandmother, Summer thought. She could defuse almost any situation, which was one of the many reasons that she also made an excellent hostess.

Not that breaking the news to her grandfather had been all that bad. Within the range of Granddad's reactions to news that he didn't want to hear, his response had been mild. It was almost as if, notwithstanding his subsequent bluster, her news hadn't come as a complete surprise to him. She wondered, too, whether she'd only imagined the flicker of respect in his eyes for a moment.

"I'll never understand Granddad."

Summer didn't realize she'd spoken aloud until Maeve said, "He has his reasons."

She looked at her grandmother. "You know the atmosphere at EPH has become downright chilly since he made it a competition among the magazines to name his successor. It's true that I haven't felt it much because Uncle Shane remains fairly easygoing, but I know Scarlet's felt the pressure at work because Aunt Finny is working harder than ever to make sure *Charisma* is at the head of the pack."

She didn't have to mention the strained relationship between her aunt Finny and her grandfather. She knew Granddad had mellowed with age, but he'd always run a tight ship. While building his empire, he'd sometimes cared more for appearances than for his family, and he'd paid for his mistakes by alienating some of his children and grandchildren.

Maeve looked sad. "I'd hoped Patrick's challenge wouldn't put additional strain on his relationship with Finny."

"But why?" Summer asked. "I just don't understand why he had to set up this rivalry within the family. It's started to pull people apart."

Maeve looked thoughtful for an instant, then said quietly, "As I said, your grandfather has his reasons for doing what he does, and he'll never back down on this one. I have faith that the family will pull through without falling apart."

Summer wasn't so sure.

She was alone again with Zeke in his hotel room and keenly aware of him. Summer tried to forget the last time she had been here.

Today he was dressed in blue jeans, a white T-shirt and an open button-down shirt. Of course, now she knew what lay beneath those clothes: hard, sculpted muscles, smooth sun-kissed skin, powerful thighs….

She yanked her mind away from her wayward thoughts. She was here to do the interview that he'd promised her and nothing else.

She knew from reading the newspapers that Zeke's publicist had issued a denial that the two of them—or, rather, he and Scarlet—were more than friends. With any luck, the whole story would soon fade away. It would, she promised herself, as long as she managed to get her interview and get out of here.

When she'd returned to work yesterday morning, after having spent the weekend torturing herself about her recent behavior, Zeke had called to schedule an interview for Tuesday afternoon.

Of course, she'd agonized over what to wear. She wanted to look professional but not prudish. She'd tossed aside her twin sets and an angora sweater, and had finally settled on a fitted silk Chinese-style jacket over black pants and half boots.

She really needed to go shopping. If not for the Chinese-style jacket that Scarlet had tossed at her at a designer sample sale, she didn't know if she'd ever have found something appropriate to wear.

"Have a seat," he said, breaking into her thoughts and making her jump. "Can I get you something to drink?"

"J-just some water. Thank you."

He smiled as he headed to the kitchenette.

Was it her imagination or was his grin tinged with wickedness? Was he remembering that the first time they'd met she'd drunk more than just water? Maybe he thought she was trying to avoid past mistakes.

When he returned, he handed her a glass of water

and took a seat in a chair perpendicular to the couch that she was sitting on.

She took a sip. It was almost a relief to be away from EPH and, instead, here interviewing Zeke. She hadn't heard from John since Friday, and she supposed he was traveling again. Scarlet was still distant, and her family's reaction to her broken engagement had ranged from shock to dismay.

"Don't you have a photographer with you?" Zeke asked, breaking into her thoughts.

"I'm taking the photos." With her free hand, she raised the case holding her camera.

He gave her a quizzical look. "You're the photographer?"

She shrugged self-consciously. "I've taken classes. It's a hobby." She put her glass down on an end table.

He gazed at her intently, and she shifted. What was he thinking?

"You look different," he said, his voice—that incredible voice—as smooth as honey and as deep and rich as chocolate.

Concentrate, Summer, she scolded herself. "Mmm, really?"

"Yeah, at the concert you were rocker girl, and at work on Friday you had a white-gloves-and-pearls retro look. Today, though, you look exotic." He cocked his head. "I'm still trying to figure out which of you is the real Summer Elliott."

Maybe she was, too. "Maybe all of them are."

He shook his head. "I don't think so. I think you're still trying to figure out who you are."

"I thought I was the one doing the interviewing," she said lightly.

His lips twitched. "Isn't an interview just a two-way conversation? Besides, the more I get to know you, the more I find you intriguing."

"Thank you—I guess."

"For instance," he went on as if he hadn't heard her, "do you *ever* wear your engagement ring?"

She thought about lying, but decided it was best to come clean. He'd probably find out the truth soon enough from the newspapers anyway. "I broke off the engagement."

She saw a flare of heat in those amazing blue eyes of his before he banked it. "You told him."

"I told him," she confirmed, then added defensively, "You're not the reason that we broke up, if that's what you're thinking. You just made me realize John and I would be making a mistake by getting married. I broke up with him before I told him what had happened between us on Thursday night."

"What did happen on Thursday night, Summer?" Zeke asked, his voice deep and smoky.

"I—I still don't know."

"It was incredible. *We* were incredible."

"Stop it. You promised—"

An Important Message from the Editors

Dear Reader,

If you'd enjoy reading romance novels with larger print that's easier on your eyes, let us send you TWO FREE HARLEQUIN PRESENTS® NOVELS in our LARGER PRINT EDITION. These books are complete and unabridged, but the type is set about 20% bigger to make it easier to read. Look inside for an actual-size sample.

By the way, you'll also get a surprise gift with your two free books!

Pam Powers

Peel off Seal and Place Inside...

FREE BOOKS

THE RIGHT WOMAN

she'd thought she was fine. It took Daniel's words and Brooke's question to make her realize she was far from a full recovery.

She'd made a start with her sister's help and she intended to go forward now. Sarah felt as if she'd been living in a darkened room and some-one had suddenly opened a door, letting in the fresh air and sunshine. She could feel its warmth slowly seeping into the coldest part of her. The feeling was liberating. She realized it was only a small step and she had a long way to go, but she was ready to face life again with Serena and her family behind her.

All too soon, they were saying goodbye and Sarah experienced a moment of sadness for all the years she and Serena had missed. But they had each other now and th't's what

She held sy c

The Harlequin Reader Service™ — Here's How It Works:

Accepting your 2 free Harlequin Presents® larger print books and gift places you under no obligation to buy anything. You may keep the books and gift and return the shipping statement marked "cancel." If you do not cancel, about a month later we'll send you 6 additional Harlequin Presents larger print books and bill you just $4.05 each in the U.S., or $4.72 each in Canada, plus 25¢ shipping & handling per book and applicable taxes if any.* That's the complete price and — compared to cover prices of $4.75 each in the U.S. and $5.50 each in Canada — it's quite a bargain! You may cancel at any time, but if you choose to continue, every month we'll send you 6 more books, which you may either purchase at the discount price or return to us and cancel your subscription.

*Terms and prices subject to change without notice. Sales tax applicable in N.Y. Canadian residents will be charged applicable provincial taxes and GST.

"What did I promise?"

She remained silent.

"I don't remember promising anything. I remember saying I wanted to see you again."

"For an interview," she clarified. He was twisting around the conversation that they'd had. "Your manager and publicist called yesterday after you did, and they peppered me with questions about the timing and substance of this interview."

"Sorry to hear that."

She looked around. "Where are they, by the way? I had the impression they wanted to be here."

His eyelids dropped, concealing his expression. "They both had things to do."

She thought that was odd, but decided not to remark on it. Instead, she brought out the tape recorder that she'd carried along with her. He was making her nervous, and the only way to avoid any more dangerous conversation was to get down to business. "Well, let's get on with the interview, don't you think?" she asked briskly. "I don't want to waste your time."

The look that he gave her was an invitation to sin. "You're not wasting my time."

A shiver chased down her spine. She cleared her throat and switched on the tape recorder. "What's your biggest challenge as a musical artist?"

He laughed. "Diving right in, aren't you?"

She raised an eyebrow.

He sighed. "Okay. The biggest challenge is to avoid repeating myself. I think that's what every artist worries about. I want my music to stay fresh and vital and to still be commercially successful."

To Summer's surprise, the interview unfolded easily after that, the conversation flowing smoothly. He talked about the success of his latest CD and his involment with Musicians for a Cure.

Eventually, she decided to move the interview to a different topic. "There haven't been any stories about you and drugs, or getting arrested, or brawling—"

"Sorry to disappoint," he quipped.

"But," she went on, "you've been described in the press as 'surly' and 'a bad boy.' How do you think you've come by your reputation?"

"Simple. I usually refuse to give interviews."

A laugh escaped her before she could stop it. "You've got different legs of an international tour for the rest of the year. What's up next?"

"Houston is next, at the end of the month, then L.A., and I'll be going abroad soon." He paused. "But I'll be staying in New York until the end of the month."

"Oh?" she said, tamping down an annoying little thrill.

"Yeah, I'll be catching up with family."

She knew from her background research that he'd grown up in New York. "I'm sure they'll be happy to see you." She turned off her tape recorder because she'd gotten what she needed for her article.

He gave her a sly grin. "Unlike you, you mean?"

She refused to take the bait. "The bio on your Web site says only that you grew up in New York."

"That's purposeful. I like my privacy." He tossed her another quick grin. "But if *you're* curious, I grew up on the Upper West Side."

She wondered whether he'd lived within a stone's throw from where she lived now.

"My father's a professor at Columbia University," he elaborated, "and my mother's a psychologist in private practice."

She tried to picture him as the son of an academic and a shrink, and failed.

He gave her a wry smile. "Yeah, I know. Hard to believe." He paused. "But not as bad as it sounds. My father's an archaeologist, so we spent most summers on digs in South America and the Middle East." He shrugged. "That probably explains why I picked a career that requires lots of travel."

"Did you always know you wanted to be a musician?" she asked.

"You mean, a rock star?" he asked mockingly, then shook his head. "No. For a while I followed the path that my parents expected of me, but a month before graduating from Columbia, I landed my first recording deal."

"What did you major in?" she asked, surprised he'd graduated from a prestigious Ivy League university. He certainly didn't have the pedigree of a typical rocker.

"Music. On and off campus. What about you?"

"English, with a minor in journalism." She added, "At NYU."

"High school?"

"Private school in the Hamptons. What about you?"

"Horace Mann," he said.

They smiled at each other until she cleared her throat. The conversation had gotten way too personal. How had that happened? "Okay, I'll just need some photos of you to accompany the article," she said.

He stood up. "Right. Where do you want me?"

She gave him a quick look. Was he coming on to her?

He just looked back at her blandly.

She stood, her digital camera in hand. "Er, somewhere bright but not in direct sunlight. Also, we'll want a backdrop that's not too busy."

"How about if I sit on the arm of that chair over there?"

She nodded. "Sounds good. Then we can take some of you standing in front of the living room wall. That'll provide a solid, off-white background."

As soon as he was ready and she'd adjusted her camera, she started snapping shots.

"Big smile," she said, and he obliged, giving her a disarming smile.

He was a natural in front of the camera, changing the angle of his head but still looking great in every shot.

She warmed as he looked at her through the camera's viewfinder. What she read in his blue eyes was enough to quicken her pulse. It was a good thing that the camera was between them, she thought, mitigating the power of his potent appeal.

All the while, she somehow continued to coax reactions from him. "Don't smile. Give me serious," she said, snapping away. "Now tilt your head down and look up at the camera." *Snap, snap.* "Now turn your head to the side and slant me a look." *Snap, snap.*

By the time he'd posed straddling the chair, and then moved to pose in front of the wall, the air in the room had become sexually charged.

"Now give me smoldering," she said unthinkingly.

He did, and she thought, *Oh, my.*

It was like experiencing vertigo. She was felt dizzy and breathless.

She lowered the camera and pretended to fiddle with it. "Okay, that's it."

He walked toward her and when he reached her, he slid his hand under her hair and around the back of her neck, exerting subtle pressure to force her head up to his.

She barely had time to close her eyes before his

lips feathered across hers. Once, twice, three times, and then he was there, claiming her mouth in a kiss that was so sweet, so deep, so satisfying that her knees nearly buckled. The hand holding her camera went limp by her side.

When he finally pulled back, she whispered, "Why did you do that?"

"Because I wanted to," he said.

She looked at him mutely.

"Because you were turning me on. Because I wanted to confirm that what I experienced on Thursday night wasn't just a fluke."

"We can't."

"Can't or shouldn't?"

"Both."

"Why? You're not engaged anymore, remember?" He rubbed his thumb across her lips. "What are you doing Friday night?"

"I've got plans. There's a party for *The Buzz* at my cousin's restaurant, Une Nuit."

"Invite me."

The letters M-I-S-T-A-K-E flashed across her mind.

"Come on," he coaxed. "Don't I deserve a thank-you for submitting to an interview? Besides, you'll be helping *The Buzz*. I'm sure the staff there would love a personal connection to another celebrity."

He was persuasive, she'd give him that.

He bent for another kiss, and she ducked. "Okay,"

she relented as she scooted past him to gather her stuff and, more importantly, to put some space between them.

For *The Buzz,* she promised herself. Only for *The Buzz.*

Seven

Une Nuit, located on Ninth Avenue on the Upper West Side, wasn't what Zeke had been expecting. He'd looked up the restaurant before coming over, so he knew it was known for its French-Asian fusion cuisine, but he was still surprised by the ambience. The decor was seductive with low red lighting, black suede seating and copper-top tables.

At Summer's insistence, they'd planned to meet at Une Nuit rather than at her place. He figured she didn't want to draw any unnecessary attention to them as a couple.

After getting a drink at the bar, he scanned the

crowd that was standing and milling about and spotted Summer laughing with some guy who looked like a male model.

Frowning, he made his way toward her, aware of the glances thrown his way. He was used to looks and whispers when he was recognized.

When Summer spied him, laughter still lurked in her eyes and she exclaimed, "Zeke, you're here!"

Apparently not a moment too soon, he thought dryly. He bent and kissed her on the cheek, grazing the corner of her lips—and staking his claim. She was dressed in black, as was he, and she looked fantastic.

As he straightened, he gave her an intimate smile. "Hi."

"Zeke, have you met Stash?" she asked, gesturing with the hand holding her wineglass.

Zeke looked Pretty Boy in the eye and noted the amusement on the other man's face. Stash? What the heck kind of name was that? And why didn't Stash go stash himself somewhere else right now?

Aloud, he said, "I haven't." He stuck out his hand. "Zeke Woodlow."

The other man grasped it. "Zee pleasure iz all mine."

Zeke almost rolled his eyes. A Frenchman? He had to compete with the lure of Stash's foreign mystique?

"Stash is the manager of Une Nuit," Summer said. "Zeke is—"

"I know who iz Zeke Woodlow, *chérie,*" Stash

said. A smile curved his lips. "I am afraid that work calls, however, so I weel leave you to your friend."

Zeke watched as Stash kissed Summer on the cheek and then sauntered off, tossing him another amused look as he went.

Stash, Zeke thought sourly, seemed like the type who could charm honey away from bees. Turning his gaze back to Summer, he asked, "You two know each other well?"

"Stash has been the manager here a long time."

Hardly reassuring, Zeke thought.

Summer beckoned to him, and with narrowed eyes, he followed her as she moved deeper into the gathered crowd.

She greeted people as she went until she was stopped by a man who looked to Zeke to be a quintessential smooth operator. The guy was around his own height of six foot one but looked to be about a decade older—perhaps in his late thirties.

Great. Was he destined to spend the whole evening batting away potential rivals?

Standing next to the dark-haired playboy type was a curvy green-eyed blonde. She gazed up at the playboy admiringly, but he hardly seemed to notice—*his* attention was directed at Summer.

Damn. He took another step forward and moved closer to Summer.

Summer looked up, seeming to realize all of a

sudden that he was still there. "Zeke," she said, "this is my uncle Shane Elliott, the editor in chief of *The Buzz*, and his executive assistant, Rachel Adler." To Shane and Rachel, she added, "This is Zeke Woodlow."

Zeke's shoulders relaxed. He needed to get a grip. His attraction to Summer was starting to drive him crazy—even if right after their interview, he'd been able to get down a major chunk of the melody and lyrics for the elusive song in his head.

Zeke shook Shane's hand and noted that Shane's grip was just as firm as his own.

"It's good to meet you," Shane said. "Summer tells me that the interview went well."

"The interviewer did her homework."

Shane laughed. "In any case, I appreciate your taking the time. We're in a heated race and every little bit helps."

The talk then shifted to a discussion of the music industry and who was topping the music charts, or would be soon, with new CDs.

When the conversation eventually ended and he and Summer had moved on, Zeke asked, "What did he mean 'we're in a heated race'?"

"I'll tell you later."

"Tell me now."

She sighed. "My grandfather, who founded Elliott Publication Holdings, recently announced that the head of whichever EPH magazine is the most profitable by the end of the year would succeed him as CEO."

Zeke whistled. "So basically he's letting his kids duke it out over who will succeed him?"

"Yes."

"So that's what made you desperate enough to try to beard the lion in his den. You were hoping an interview with me would help the home team."

He watched her shrug. "I did it for myself *and* for *The Buzz*. I'm just hoping Granddad's challenge doesn't tear this family apart."

Zeke grimaced. "It's at times like this that I appreciate growing up an only child." He gave her a wry smile. "No matter what, the parents still have only me."

"And you still have them."

The look in her eyes made him stop. He'd done some digging into her background on the Internet, and surprisingly, while there'd been plenty of mentions of her grandparents and assorted other Elliott relatives, there'd been none connecting her to her parents.

Before he could ask, however, she said, "My parents died together in a plane crash when I was ten."

"God, I'm sorry," he said.

"I've had fifteen years to learn to cope, but, you know, the hurt never completely goes away."

Before he could respond to that, their conversation was interrupted by a man Summer introduced as her cousin Bryan, the owner of Une Nuit.

"Stash sent me over," Bryan said before Summer could say any more. "He told me that he'd run into the two of you together by the door."

From the way Bryan pronounced the word *together* and from the look in his eyes, Zeke could tell he'd come over to check things out himself.

Doing some sizing up of his own, Zeke estimated that Bryan was about his own age—twenty-eight. In contrast to Shane, however, there seemed nothing laid-back about this Elliott cousin. If anything, Bryan seemed to be constantly watchful, taking in everything and giving nothing away. He was like a panther ready to pounce.

Zeke looked Bryan in the eye as they shook hands, and a certain recognition and mutual respect passed between them.

"Bryan has the perfect life," Summer joked.

"Really?" Zeke asked, looking from Summer to Bryan and back.

"Yes," Summer said, throwing her cousin a teasing look. "He has this fantastic bachelor pad above the restaurant that lets him just fall out of bed and go to work. Not only that, but he's got a job that keeps him well away from EPH and us other Elliotts. Or, I should say, one Elliott in particular, namely my grandfather. And on top of it all, Bryan gets to travel to fantastic places for the restaurant."

Interesting, Zeke thought. Not only was the statement revealing about Bryan, but it was intriguing that Summer thought the perfect job was *away* from EPH.

"Summer's exaggerating," Bryan said.

"No, I'm not."

"Where do you travel for the restaurant?" Zeke asked.

Bryan shrugged. "Europe mainly. Paris."

"I was in Paris just a month ago. What did you think of—?"

"Excuse me, will you?" Bryan said suddenly. "I just spotted someone I've been trying to catch up with all evening."

Strange, Zeke thought, watching Bryan's departing back. He got the distinct impression that Bryan wanted to avoid talking about his travels.

Zeke watched as another guy who'd also been observing Bryan's departure turned back now and said, "I see you've met the clan's International Man of Mystery."

Turning to Summer, the guy gave her a peck on the cheek and said, "Hey, honey. Long time no see."

"Zeke, this is—"

"Let me guess," he said dryly. "Your cousin." The guy bore a striking resemblance to Bryan. They shared the same coloring of jet-black hair and blue eyes. In personality, however, this cousin seemed as smooth and laid-back as Shane.

"Cullen Elliott," the man before him said, his eyes glinting. "I'm Bryan's younger brother." Holding up his thumb and index finger a half an inch apart, he added, "But only by that much."

"Cullen is the director of sales for *Snap,*" Summer supplied.

Zeke feigned shock. "You're from the rival camp? What are you doing here?"

Cullen grinned. "I'm invited everywhere." He added, "So Summer's filled you in on the family rivalry, has she?"

"Yeah," he said. Turning to Summer and jerking a finger at Cullen, he asked, "If he's here, where's Scarlet? Doesn't she work for an EPH magazine, too?"

Zeke watched Summer frown. "Scarlet decided not to come. She went skiing with friends this weekend."

Cullen turned to him and raised an eyebrow. "I saw the piece about you and Scarlet in the *Post,*" he teased. "Are you wondering if you're out with the right sister?"

If only Cullen knew, Zeke thought. Beside him, he noticed that Summer froze for a second, then pasted a lighthearted smile on her face.

"Don't listen to Cullen," Summer said, swatting her cousin playfully. "He's broken more hearts than I can count."

"Yup, that's me," Cullen said, obviously playing along, though Zeke noticed a shadow flit across his face. "I'm giving Shane a run for his money for the title of Playboy Elliott."

They talked to Cullen a little more, then Zeke suggested to Summer that they head to the bar and refresh their drinks.

When he'd asked the bartender for a bourbon on the rocks for himself and another glass of white wine for Summer, he turned to her and said with dry amusement, "I've run the gauntlet for you tonight with your relatives."

"They're just curious," Summer responded. "They know I broke off the engagement to John, and now, tonight, I show up with you."

"Did you tell them that it was you and not Scarlet at the Waldorf?"

"No, but they're curious nevertheless."

"Do they have anything to be curious about?" he couldn't resist countering.

She cast him a sidelong look. "Not anymore."

He noted, however, that, when their shoulders accidentally brushed, she moved away self-consciously. She was clearly not as cool and collected as she wanted to appear.

He handed her drink to her and took a sip of his own. "I like your cousins. They're interesting characters."

"Interesting?"

"More than they seem," he elaborated.

She tilted her head inquiringly.

"Bryan and Cullen seem like they have a few secrets. Bryan in particular."

Summer looked doubtful. "You know, Cullen was joking when he said Bryan was the International Man of Mystery. It's just that, more than most of the rest of us Elliotts, Bryan has a separate life away from the family."

He arched a brow. "Something tells me there's more to it than that."

Summer looked skeptical, but then smiled. "I've known them my whole life and, believe me, there's never been anything mysterious about them. Bryan is a restaurateur at heart, and Cullen...Cullen is exactly what he said he is. He's a magnet for women."

Zeke decided not to push the point further, though he remained unconvinced Bryan and Cullen were as uncomplicated as baby cousin Summer thought they were.

He followed Summer to a buffet that had been set up at the back of the restaurant and they helped themselves to items such as fried Kumamoto oysters, crab and avocado millefeuilles, and a lobster and melon salad with Asian pear and Thai mango dressing.

Later, Cullen joined them again, and Zeke met a few more of Summer's coworkers, who all seemed curious about him.

Eventually, however, they were left alone at a

corner table, and an awkward silence reigned—a novel situation for him where women were concerned.

Slowly, though, he succeeded in drawing her out. They talked about the places that he'd traveled to, and he regaled her with stories about strange and unusual fans and even weirder tabloid headlines.

They discovered that they both knew how to speak Spanish well and French badly, that they loved Malta in the summertime, and that they preferred their Mexican food really spicy. They debated whether they'd had better skiing in Vale or the Alps, and which were the best places to go on St. Bart's.

"So," he finally joked, "what're your musical tastes? Who do you like?"

"They're all dead."

He laughed. He supposed he shouldn't have been surprised. "Classical?"

She took a sip of her wine. "Yes, and oldies. Sinatra. Nat King Cole."

"Are you just being diplomatic and trying not to admit you prefer my competition?" he teased.

She looked at him from beneath her lashes. "If I did, would you mind?"

Realizing that she was flirting with him, he banked his satisfaction. "I'd be heartbroken, but I'd console myself with the thought that we're both Beethoven fans."

A smile tugged at her mouth. "I enjoyed your concerts. You're very good."

"Only very good?" he teased again.

She looked into his eyes. "Compelling," she said softly.

As he continued to look into her eyes, he felt himself go up in smoke. Man, she had an effect on him.

He decided to let her—and himself—off the hook. "Actually, chances are I'll be leaving the performing behind sooner rather than later."

He could tell he'd surprised her. "Really?"

"Yeah, I see myself concentrating on songwriting instead." He looked around. The crowd had thinned a bit, though the party was still going strong.

"Are you ready to leave?" she asked.

"Yeah." He looked at her. "I'm ready, are you?"

It was a loaded question, and he knew it, but he wanted her badly. Being near her and holding back was torture.

"Yes," she said, "let's go." She gave no indication that she'd taken him at other than face value.

They wound their way to the front door, saying good-night to people on the way, and he retrieved her coat and his jacket from the attendant at the cloak room.

Fortunately, Shane and Cullen were nowhere to be found. Bryan, on the other hand, just tossed him a significant look that said Zeke had a modicum of his trust and shouldn't do anything to waste it. Zeke gave him the barest of nods that said the message had been delivered and noted.

He held the front door open for Summer, and when they got outside the restaurant, he pulled a baseball cap out of his jacket pocket and pulled it low over his eyes.

She looked at him questioningly.

"Keeps me from being recognized by paparazzi," he explained. "Can I get you a cab?"

"No, thank you," she said. "Home is just a few blocks away."

"I'll walk with you, then."

She hesitated for a second. "Okay."

Eight

She was burning up. It was crazy, of course. It was only thirty degrees outside. But beneath her cashmere coat and underneath her wraparound top, she was burning up.

And it was all due to the man beside her.

Zeke.

Her lover.

When they arrived at the Elliott townhouse, Summer watched as Zeke looked up at the huge gray structure, taking it in.

She was used to people being impressed by the place that she and Scarlet used as a weekday residence and that her grandparents used when they were in town.

She tried to see it through his eyes, as if for the first time. The three-story mansion boasted white trim and was set ten feet back from the street, shielded from curious passersby by a black wrought iron gate covered in ivy.

Zeke looked at her. "Your grandfather wasted no words in making a statement, I'll say that for him."

His insightfulness surprised her. Most visitors' observations ended with the physical structure before them. "Granddad started the EPH empire," she said. "On his way up, I think appearances were very important to him."

"Yeah."

"Jealous?"

A smile quivered at his lips and he glanced at her. "More like envious of his privacy." He added, "And feeling like an idiot now for thinking you'd be impressed by my suite at the Waldorf."

She flushed. She didn't like being reminded of how she'd misled him that night, but he didn't look angry now, only as if he was enjoying teasing her.

Still, now that they'd arrived at the townhouse, an awkwardness fell over her. Trying to cast off the feeling, she heard herself ask, "Would you like to see the inside?"

"Sure."

As they made their way up to the front door and

inside, she had time to rue her impulsive offer. She should've said goodbye outside.

Should've, could've, hadn't.

Instead, after they had deposited her coat and his jacket and cap in the front hall, she showed him around. The house was quiet because of the late hour, the few servants asleep or gone for the day.

She was very aware of him behind her as they made their way from the grand entry hall, with its impressive stained glass skylight, to the library and then on to the dining room and living room. She showed him the family room and kitchen, and they looked out at the back porch, which overlooked a private garden.

Eventually, he followed her up to the next level, where bedrooms for family and guests were located, and then to the top floor, where she and Scarlet had sleeping quarters.

Finally, he stood in the open doorway of her bedroom.

Trying to gauge his reaction, she babbled, "And this is my room. It's been redecorated over the years. Fortunately, Scarlet and I never had to share a bathroom. I'm not sure our relationship would have survived otherwise."

She looked around at the white-and-cream color scheme that contrasted dramatically with the antique cherrywood furniture, and at her brass bed with its matelassé cover.

What was he thinking? Too cozy?

He said nothing, just looked around, and she stopped fidgeting.

Finally, he murmured, "Very feminine."

He strolled in and stopped by the closed laptop and paperwork on her desk. Looking down, he asked, "You've started writing up our interview?"

"Yes." She walked over to him. She'd forgotten she'd left her draft sitting out.

He picked up some sheets of paper and cast her a curious look. "Do you mind?"

"No—I mean, no, I don't mind." She gave a nervous laugh. "As long as you don't expect the right to censor it."

He quirked a brow. "Don't worry," he murmured. "Given all the stuff that's already been written about me, I doubt I'll be shocked."

She waited nervously as he read.

She'd labored over every word of the article so far. And every word had brought back in stunning detail thoughts of him and of that night at the Waldorf.

She'd toiled over how to describe him without sounding trite or love struck. *Zeke Woodlow, soul of an artist, body of a sex symbol,* she'd written before deleting the words. She'd called herself ridiculous and more, then had stared at the blank computer screen for ages.

Finally, she'd decided to open with the heart of the matter: a quote from Zeke himself on striving to keep his music fresh and relevant.

Just then, he broke into her thoughts. "Very good," he said. "I like it."

"Really?" Realizing she'd sounded embarrassingly surprised, she tried again, "I mean, really?"

A smile played at his lips. "Yeah, really. I have just one criticism."

"Oh?"

He put the article down. "It needs more research."

"I'm not sure there's anything else I need to know."

He moved closer until he was standing within scant inches of her, and she felt her breath catch in her throat.

"Are you sure?" he murmured. "Because there are lots of things I need to know about you."

Their sexually tinged banter was causing her skin to prickle with awareness. "Such as?" she whispered.

His hand came up to cup the side of her face, the pad of his thumb tracing over her lips. "Such as whether your skin is always so soft." He drew her closer and bent his head. "Such as whether your mouth is always as kissable as it looks," he whispered against her lips.

His mouth fit over hers expertly, and soon she was lost in the same sensations that had swirled between them that first night at the Waldorf.

She clung to him until he lifted his head and looked down at her, his eyes lingering on the deep *V* created by her wraparound top. "I like what you're wearing tonight," he said in a low voice.

"I went shopping," she confessed. She'd finally nabbed some time and headed to the stores, determined to have something to wear for tonight that sent the right message. She hadn't spent too much time analyzing why it mattered so much what she wore.

"Very sophisticated."

"Maybe it's the emergence of the new Summer Elliott," she joked.

"If it is, I'd be only too happy to help with the process in any way I can," he said seductively.

She felt a strange fluttering in her stomach. This dance of desire that they were engaged in was still new territory for her. "We were talking about the interview."

"Yes…and research."

"Are you trying to seduce me?"

"If I am, is it working?" His gaze lingered on her chest, where her nipples pressed against the material of her top. "You seem kind of turned on."

"You're not really my type." Was she trying to convince him or herself? "Everyone that I've dated has had conservatively short hair." They'd also had desk jobs. A closet full of business suits. *They hadn't been rebels.*

He laughed. "Learn to live dangerously."

Did she dare?

"And you're definitely my type," he teased.

She looked at him disbelievingly.

"Authentic," he clarified. "Fresh and natural and lovely."

She looked into his gorgeous blue eyes and felt her self-control slip, but she said, "For once, I'd like to think of you outside a haze of desire."

He laughed. "Why? Some people say the luckiest ones are those that never emerge from the haze."

Maybe he was right, she thought. Ever since the night at the Waldorf, a question had lingered: Who was that passionate woman who'd tangled the sheets with Zeke Woodlow? An aberration? Or a part of herself that the sensible Summer Elliott had kept bottled up, fearing to let loose?

She wanted to find out, and Zeke seemed all too willing to oblige her.

He shifted closer at the same time that she took a tiny step toward him. She fit seamlessly into his embrace, and mouth met mouth.

Summer felt Zeke's hand fit over her breast and rub her nipple, bringing it to a peak and making her want him all the more. When his lips moved away from hers, he feathered kisses over her eyelids, along the side of her face, and down to the hollow of her throat.

She tugged at his crewneck shirt until it came free

from where it was tucked into his jeans. He finally obliged her by yanking it over his head.

Not waiting for an invitation, she trailed her fingertips over his chest, feeling his hard muscles flex under her touch.

When he stilled abruptly and cursed, she raised her eyes to his. "What's wrong?"

"I didn't bring any protection."

"I have some."

"Why, Ms. Elliott," he drawled, "were you planning to seduce me?"

She batted her eyelashes at him. "Not until tonight, but I happen to know Scarlet has some condoms in her bathroom. Scarlet's a better-safe-than-sorry kind of girl."

Sure enough, Summer located an unopened pack in her sister's bathroom cabinet. As she returned to her own bedroom, she thought she heard Zeke humming. Walking into the room again, she discovered he'd lit some of the candles. The faint scent of roses hung in the air.

"Now, where were we?" he asked coming toward her. He took a foil packet from her hand and tossed it on the night table.

He took her in his arms and kissed the corner of her mouth, pulling at the tie of her wraparound top until it came undone. Pushing the delicate material off her shoulders, he exposed her breasts, encased in a lacy bra.

He looked up at her, his lips quirking. "I'll say this for you. You've got fantastic taste in lingerie."

She smiled, embarrassed. The truth was, she'd taken to heart Scarlet's advice from the night of the concert: dress sexy and you'll feel sexy. So, she'd gone out and bought more sexy underwear. "It's a recent development."

"Well, hurray for small changes." He cupped her breasts and stroked them, arousing her.

"Zeke…"

"Yeah?"

Take me. I've got to have you inside me. She longed to give him the kind of sexy words that he'd whispered to her on the first night they'd made love, but she found she couldn't speak.

"What do you want, Summer?" he asked, his voice low and seductive. "Tell me."

"Kiss my breasts."

"Mmm," he said, his eyes hooded. "Kiss them? You mean like this?" He bent and placed open-mouthed kisses at the cleavage revealed by her bra. "Is that what you want?"

"No," she said, her voice tinged with frustration. He knew what she wanted.

He seemed to pretend to consider. "No?"

All at once, she knew what she had to do. Two could play at this game. He was teasing her, and suddenly there was every reason to shed her inhibitions.

Keeping her eyes steady on his, she took a step back.

"Where are you going?" he asked.

"Nowhere," she said seductively. "Why don't you have a seat, Zeke?"

His eyes widened a fraction, but he sat down on the bed.

"Comfortable?" she asked as she went to the bedside lamp and dimmed the lighting.

"Yeah."

"I hope you like jazz," she said as she turned on soft music. "Some people say it puts them in the mood. Do you agree?"

"Come here and find out."

A thrill coursed through her at his words. She moved toward him, and, while she did so, she unclasped her bra and let it fall to the floor. Reaching him, she pushed him back against the bed until he rested on his elbows, and then she straddled him.

His face registered surprise and then delight. "Now that you've got me, what are you going to do with me?"

She bent and kissed him, deeply and languorously. When she pulled back, she said, "Kiss me." She gazed into his eyes. "I want you to kiss my breasts. I want you to do all those wonderfully erotic things that you did that night in your hotel room."

He sat up. "With pleasure."

She guided him to her and when his mouth closed over her breast, she sighed, her fingers tangling in his hair and her eyes fluttering shut. He played first with one breast and then with the other, until she thought she couldn't stand any more.

Clasping her, he tumbled her down onto the bed and came down beside her, his leg wedged between the two of hers. She could feel his erection pressing into her hip.

He kissed her, making love to her with his mouth, his hands caressing her while hers stole up and down his arms, playing over hard muscles.

When the air between them had become charged to a fever pitch and they were both breathing deeply, he levered himself off the bed.

He stripped the remaining clothes from her and then shed his own jeans and shoes.

She surveyed him unabashedly. He was aroused and gorgeous.

"Feel free to touch," he said.

She wanted to.

She sat up and reached out, taking his erection in her hand and stroking him.

He closed his eyes, his breathing becoming deep and harsh.

When he groaned, she bent and took him in her mouth.

"Ah, Summer," he sighed, his voice throaty.

She'd never felt so powerful and sexy.

When she finally pulled away, Zeke came down

beside her on the bed, a helpless laugh escaping him. "Wow. That felt good."

She smiled at him, suddenly a bit shy.

He looked at her closely. "What's this? Embarrassment from my seductress?" He cocked his head. "Maybe I should really give you something to blush about."

Moving over her, he kissed and stroked his way down her body, leaving her hot and aroused and wanting. When he reached her inner thighs, she moaned and tried to clamp them shut.

"Shh," he soothed.

He took his time until his questing mouth went to the very core of her, which was warm and wet and wanting him.

Summer felt the world close around her like a warm cocoon. There was only Zeke and the wonderful things that he was doing to her…until the universe exploded behind her eyes and she shook with ripples of pleasure.

When she finally returned to earth, she heard the sound of ripping foil, and then Zeke was beside her again, taking her into his arms.

He held her and kissed her, and this time his entry was smooth and uninterrupted, though he seemed to go slowly to give her time to adjust to him.

Once he was inside her, he rolled over so that she lay on top of him.

She looked down at him in surprise, the curtain of her hair shielding them from their surroundings.

"Take me where you want to go, Summer," he said huskily. "You're in control."

She hesitated for a second, then moved experimentally. His responding groan was all the encouragement she needed.

She let him guide her in setting up a rhythm, following him as he quickened the pace. She watched as his eyes closed and his muscles became taut, his face tensing with pleasure.

She closed her eyes, too, concentrating on the pleasure building between them.

When her climax came, she gasped, spasmed and then stilled as Zeke grasped her hips and thrust into her.

Zeke groaned and, a split second later, joined her in going over the edge to sweet oblivion.

She fell against him then, and he held her.

"Ah, Summer, you do it for me every time," he said, stroking her hair. "You are so passionate."

"I've never thought of myself as passionate," she said, her voice muffled against his shoulder.

"You're kidding."

She shook her head, then raised it to look at him. "John and I never shared much passion."

He shook his head. "Well, take it from me. You're one of the most responsive women I've ever met. I just can't believe you remained a virgin this long."

"It was all part of the five-year plan."

"Huh?"

"The five-year plan," she repeated. "I drew up a life plan, and part of it called for getting married by twenty-six."

He laughed, then asked curiously, "And what else did it say?"

"Oh, you know, the usual stuff. Aim to get promoted to management by thirty. Have a baby." Somehow, giving voice to her goals seemed like confessing something embarrassing.

"You can't live life by a neat plan."

"It's important to have goals," she said defensively.

"Yeah, but not when they interfere with examining your evolving feelings. Sometimes plans can get in the way of getting what you really want."

"You sound like an expert."

He grinned. "You can take it from me. I'm the son of a psychologist, and I'm also someone who gets paid big bucks for singing about emotions."

"Yes, I noticed. I thought I heard you humming something under your breath a little while ago before we were, ah, otherwise occupied. I didn't recognize the tune. What was it?"

"Nothing," he said obliquely. "Just a song that I kind of know."

"Hmm," she said, running her foot along his leg.

His hand clamped down on her moving leg and

stilled her, his face taking on a seductive intensity. "On the other hand, I don't just *kind of* know you."

As he pressed her into the bed, she laughed breathlessly and gave herself up to tonight, for once not thinking about tomorrow.

Nine

The next morning, Summer woke up feeling happier and more content than she could recall being in a long time. She looked across at the man lying asleep next to her.

Zeke.

She'd never before woken up next to a man. She wondered why she never had, and yet she knew how she was feeling now was due to Zeke himself.

Looking at him, she itched for her camera so she could snap his picture. In repose, unguarded, his features relaxed, he looked even more heart-stoppingly handsome than on stage.

A part of her couldn't believe *the* Zeke Woodlow had taken an interest in her. She knew he couldn't be attracted to her for her money, since he was very wealthy in his own right.

She recalled the events of last night and flushed. They'd fallen asleep and woken up to make love twice more during the night. After the last time, Zeke had sung her to sleep. Just thinking of it now, she felt warm and cherished all over again.

She was pleased he'd liked the write-up that she'd done of their interview. She'd walk on hot coals before she'd admit it to anyone, but she'd played back the tape of their interview repeatedly, just to hear the sound of his voice.

She watched as Zeke opened his eyes and smiled, rolling on his side toward her and stroking her with his hand. "Hi."

She smiled back at him. "Hi."

He pulled her toward him and nuzzled her neck. She laughed and squirmed, and soon there was no more talking.

Much later, he asked, "Any plans for the weekend?" He waggled his eyebrows. "Spending it in bed, I'm hoping."

She laughed. "Actually, I usually go to The Tides."

At his confused look, she added, "My grandparents' estate in the Hamptons. It's where Scarlet and I were raised after my parents died."

His hand caressed her thigh. "Take me along."

"I couldn't!"

The words were out of her mouth before she had a chance to think. Yet, of course she couldn't bring him to The Tides! Last night Une Nuit, and now The Tides? She'd be flaunting him right after her breakup with John.

He cocked his head and gave her a look of mock offense. "What's the matter? I'm good enough to sleep with but not good enough to be seen with?"

"Isn't that my line?" she responded. At the moment she still had to figure out how to sneak him out of the townhouse without alerting any of the servants. Fortunately, there was a secondary entrance from the outside directly to the living quarters that she shared with Scarlet. She just had to get downstairs to retrieve his jacket and cap, which they'd left in the foyer last night, and sneak back up.

Zeke just continued to look at her in amusement, and she wondered for a second whether he'd read her mind.

"Anyway," she asked, "aren't you busy? Don't you have things that you need to be doing this weekend?"

He smiled. "Nope. I'm all yours."

"We'll have to take separate bedrooms," she warned, weakening despite herself. "My grandparents are traditional." She didn't add that, of course, she wouldn't give him the room that John used to stay in. *That* would be a little much all around.

He gave her an intimate smile. "I can be fun out of bed, too."

She heated. "You're incorrigible."

So it was that, later that day, they pulled into The Tides' parking garage. Because they'd gotten a late start and had had to swing by the Waldorf, it was already after lunchtime when they arrived.

As they walked along the breezeway that connected the garage with the rest of the mansion, she watched Zeke look around, then arch a brow. "Even more impressive than the townhouse."

She shrugged half-apologetically. "To me, The Tides has always been just home."

"Some home," he said as they walked into the house.

They dumped their overnight bags in their rooms, and Summer was relieved when she was told by Olive that her grandparents were out and would not be back until dinner. At least she didn't have to deal with those introductions just yet.

"How is Aunt Karen?" she asked Olive.

"Michael brought her into the city to see her doctors. The both of them are not expected back until Monday."

Uh-oh. She'd been hoping her aunt and uncle would be around to act as a buffer between Zeke and her grandparents.

Olive served them a quick late lunch, and afterward Summer said to Zeke, "Come on, I'll show you around the estate."

They went back to their rooms for jackets to guard against the blustery March weather. On the way out Summer grabbed her camera and slipped it into her pocket. She always left one of her digital cameras in her room at The Tides. She liked to amuse herself on weekends by taking pictures of the surrounding landscape, playing with light and shadows and capturing the changing seasons.

Outside, they toured the grounds together, taking in the pool house, the helicopter landing pad that her grandfather used when commuting to work in Manhattan, and the site of the English rose garden that Maeve lovingly tended and that bloomed in warmer weather.

Finally, they stopped at the top of hand-carved stone stairs that led down from a bluff to a private beach and boat dock.

Summer drew the camera from her pocket.

She saw Zeke grin as he spotted it.

"What's so funny?" she asked.

"You. I still think you're more suited to be in front of the camera than behind it."

"Oh." She flushed. "I thought that was just a line you were giving me when we were in your dressing room after the concert."

He arched a brow. "Distrustful sort, huh?" He shook his head. "No, I really meant it. With your coloring, you're model material."

"Will you pose for me?" she asked, skirting a subject she wanted to avoid.

"I thought you'd want to capture the landscape."

She shrugged. "I often do, but today I want to photograph you. You have an interesting face." A compelling face. She didn't want to admit just how fascinated she was by it. By him.

He gave her a wicked grin. "Okay, I'll pose for you. I like where this led last time."

She remembered, too. It had led to kissing and would probably have led to much more if she hadn't fled after their interview. *Careful, Summer.*

Soon, though, she was snapping photos of him from different angles, first as he looked out at the water, and then as he stood on the stone steps.

"Did you ever do photo sessions with John?" he asked when she was done.

"No," she answered, then realized how that sounded. She lowered her camera and busied herself with shutting it off and putting it away.

"Hey," Zeke said as he came back up the steps to join her, "I want to see how those pictures turned out."

"I'll e-mail them to you."

She was troubled by what she'd admitted to Zeke—and to herself. She'd never been fascinated by John's face, had never had a compulsive urge to snap his picture.

Good grief, what was wrong with her? She'd

nearly convinced herself to marry a man who'd really been not much more than a good friend. On the other hand, maybe it was her current fascination with Zeke that was abnormal.

When she looked up, she caught Zeke gazing at her thoughtfully.

"It's okay if you find me more fascinating than you do other men," he teased.

He saw too much, she thought with chagrin. "Let's get back."

Later that evening, as she sat across the dining table from Zeke, Summer realized dinner was going to be as much of a trial as she'd thought. Olive had informed her grandparents that Summer had brought a "male friend" along with her.

Summer had started to count the number of times that her grandfather's eyebrows had risen and fallen with suspicion, and now she wondered if civility would hold sway at least until the end of the meal.

Even her grandparents had heard of Zeke Woodlow and, of course, her grandfather was no fool. If her cousins had seemed to sense there was more to her relationship with Zeke than met the eye, then certainly Patrick Elliott wouldn't be fooled. Last weekend she'd announced her broken engagement, and this weekend she was showing up at The Tides with a different man in tow.

At that thought, she caught her grandfather's penetrating look and nearly winced as she got a good idea of his thoughts: *Well, Summer, my girl, these are the sorts of shenanigans that I'd have expected out of your sister and not from you.*

Zeke cleared his throat, breaking the uncomfortable silence that had descended. "So, Summer tells me you're in the process of choosing a successor. Do you already have big plans for your retirement?"

Summer groaned inwardly. The word *retirement* didn't exist in her grandfather's vocabulary. Not really, and certainly not as applied to him.

She wondered why Zeke would bring up a touchy subject. She'd already told him how the competition among magazines was exacerbating family tensions. She tossed him a quelling look that he either didn't see or refused to acknowledge.

Summer watched as her grandfather leisurely finished buttering a roll and took his time answering. She knew from experience that one of her grandfather's techniques for making his targets uncomfortable was to draw out the silence.

Zeke, however, appeared to remain completely at ease. It was she who felt like squirming.

When Patrick finally looked up, he said, "Some of us never really stop working. For others, though, the party never seems to end." He bit into his roll.

Argh, Summer thought.

She watched as Zeke took his time chewing his food and swallowing. "Yes, sir. That's all too true. I'm glad we fall into the same camp on that score."

Patrick huffed, as though he couldn't believe Zeke had the audacity to claim that he—the up-by-his-bootstraps, self-made founder of a publishing empire—had anything in common with a bad-boy rock star.

Summer noticed her grandmother hide a smile. Well, at least Gram seemed to be rooting for the underdog.

Patrick stopped eating and addressed Zeke. "You mentioned that your parents are a professor and a psychologist. Do they approve of your career choice?"

"They weren't too happy at first, but they realized I was entitled to pursue my own dreams. How about yours?"

Summer thought she heard her grandfather say something under his breath that sounded suspiciously like "insolent pup." She wanted to crawl under the table, or at least throw her napkin over her head.

Maeve appeared to catch the pleading look that Summer sent her and said, "When Patrick first came calling, my father disliked him intensely."

"Then I'm glad he's only continuing a family tradition," Zeke said.

Maeve looked greatly amused, while Patrick lowered his eyebrows.

To Patrick, Zeke added, "I'm like you. Ambitious, hard-working and willing to start at the bottom and work my way up in a field in which I had no connections."

Patrick studied Zeke thoughtfully. "But still with time to dally, it seems. First with one granddaughter, now with the other, eh?"

At Summer's gasp, her grandfather turned to her and added, "Don't look at me like that, my girl. I'm still able to read, and, yes, news of Scarlet's appearance with Zeke in the *Post* did make its way back to me. I may need reading glasses, but I'm not dead yet."

"That was me, not Scarlet, Granddad!"

The minute the words were out of her mouth, Summer regretted them.

Patrick sat back, a curiously satisfied look on his face.

Summer flushed. "I mean—"

Zeke looked Patrick in the eye. "There is no explanation."

Summer recovered enough to add, "I still meant what I said last weekend. I realized that John and I wouldn't suit, that we're too alike, so I called off the engagement."

"Your grandfather understands," Maeve interjected. "After all, there was a time when he was young and impetuous himself."

"Never," Patrick declared.

"Why," Maeve continued, as if she hadn't heard her husband, "my father swore that Patrick was heading for the shortest courtship on record."

Maeve then steered the conversation to a safer topic and asked Olive to bring in some fresh fruit.

Summer was relieved when dinner wrapped up soon after that. Afterward, she sat with Maeve in the small tearoom, which was done up with chintz-upholstered furniture, and sipped some herbal tea from a porcelain cup. Her grandfather and Zeke had disappeared into the library, and Summer worried about their conversation.

"I think Patrick likes him," Maeve said.

Summer jerked up her head to look at her grandmother. "You're kidding. How can you tell?"

Maeve gave her a fond little smile. "Zeke refused to be cowed. He put me in mind of Patrick nearly sixty years ago when he came to Ireland and courted me."

Summer mulled over her grandmother's comment, and later that night, when she finally caught Zeke alone, she said, "I did try to warn you about Granddad."

Zeke laughed. "His bark is worse than his bite."

"What did you talk about in the library?" she asked curiously.

"We smoked cigars and shot the breeze. He showed me his impressive collection of first editions." He added with a wink, "Don't worry, I like him."

Her eyebrows shot upward in surprise, but Zeke just laughed again.

* * *

On Wednesday night, Zeke picked up Summer at work in his rented sports car. They'd made plans to eat at Peter Luger Steak House in the Williamsburg section of Brooklyn, just over the bridge from Manhattan, and then take in a photography exhibit at an art gallery in nearby Fort Greene, which was known as an artists' haven from Manhattan's high rents.

He'd never met anyone quite like Summer, Zeke reflected. She was a bundle of contradictions. An heiress with few pretensions and not a few insecurities. A throwback to another era, but one who had career ambitions. A recent ex-virgin who could send him from relaxed to heavily aroused in less than a minute.

Maybe that was why he found her so fascinating.

He glanced over at her now as they strolled the streets of Fort Greene. She had on a short, fitted leather jacket and, under it, a black-and-white striped top that dipped low and was gathered enticingly between her pert breasts. He hadn't been able to stop his gaze from wandering back there again and again during their recently ended dinner.

In fact, he'd had to stop himself from whisking her back to his hotel room in order to spend the evening in bed, engaging in hot and satisfying sex.

"Here we are," she said, smiling and turning to him, interrupting his thoughts.

He looked at the storefront behind her. The store windows were draped with red velvet curtains that shielded the inside, and there were no signs indicating what lay within except for a discreetly placed plaque beside the front door with the words Tentra Gallery in black.

As he soon discovered, however, the space inside was light, airy and loft-like, with a second-floor accessible by elevator. Photographs hung on the walls, each marked by a nameplate and a brief description.

The gallery had attracted a sizable but not over-whelming crowd. And because he didn't want to be recognized, he kept his baseball cap on.

He and Summer started at one end of the gallery and, taking their time, gazed at each photograph individually.

"Remind me again of why we're here," he murmured.

She laughed softly. "Because Oren Levitt is a good friend and one of the photographers whose work is being shown."

"How good a friend?"

She cast him a sidelong look. "Jealous?"

"Do I have reason to be?"

She looked at him from beneath her lashes. "No." Then she added, "Oren's engaged to his longtime girlfriend."

"Good." Irrational relief washed over him. He couldn't recall ever being this possessive—or passionate—about a woman before.

Just then, a lanky guy whose look was all grunge approached, accompanied by a petite woman with dyed black hair and heavy eyeliner.

Summer made the introductions, and Zeke gave a nod of acknowledgment to Oren and his fiancée, Tabitha.

Both seemed impressed and enthusiastic to be meeting *the* Zeke Woodlow, and, as far as Zeke could tell, the only awkwardness came when Oren asked Summer about how John was doing and she had to divulge their recent breakup. If Oren and Tabitha wondered about Zeke's own relationship with Summer, however, they kept their thoughts to themselves.

After Oren and Tabitha had moved on to greet some new arrivals, Zeke glanced down at Summer and said, "Not exactly the type of friends that I'd have thought a debutante like you would have."

She arched a brow. "Are you saying you think I'm a snob?"

"I'm just surprised, that's all. Until recently, you were all pearls and cashmere, and you've still got the posture of a comportment-school grad and the manners for afternoon tea with royalty."

Summer sighed. "I met Oren in photography

class. I met a lot of different people in my photography classes. I *like* meeting different types of people."

"And yet," he mused, "you were about to marry a guy who's apparently just like you."

Turning, he sauntered over to the nearest photo on the wall, leaving her to mull over that observation.

He noticed that she said nothing, but eventually she walked over to join him.

It seemed to Zeke, from what was on display, that Oren liked to do funky portraits. His work was sort of a cross between the photos of Annie Leibovitz and the art of Andy Warhol.

When they made their way up to the second floor, Zeke discovered more of Oren's photographs.

"This is some of Oren's earlier work," Summer said, then added with a frown, "I didn't know he'd have some of these on display tonight."

Zeke spared her a glance as he walked toward the nearest photographs. One was of a clown, another of someone dressed as Marie Antoinette, the ill-fated queen of France.

Turning a corner, he saw other photos hung on the back of a flat pillar—and was brought up short.

Daphne.

It was the same woman who graced the photo that now hung in his mansion back in L.A. The same woman who glorified his dreams. He could swear it was.

Except the woman in this photograph was dressed in a Victorian ball gown, her hair in an elaborate twist on top of her head, her face made-up and partially obscured by a fan.

His eyes went to the nameplate accompanying the photo: "Daphne Victoria."

"What's wrong?" Summer asked as she joined him, glancing at his face and then at the photo on the wall.

He heard her sharp intake of breath before she looked back at him.

With Summer and Daphne now side by side, Zeke found he could finally really compare the two. The pale-green eyes were the same, but as with "Daphne at Play," the hair of the woman in the photo was a couple shades darker than Summer's own auburn.

"The resemblance is uncanny, isn't it?" he murmured. He tore his eyes away from the photo and looked at Summer. "Are the photos on display tonight for sale?"

"I suppose so."

"Good." He nodded at the photo in front of him. "I'll take that one." He glanced around. "In fact, if there are any others like it, I'll take those, too."

"Zeke."

He turned back to face Summer, who stood chewing on her lower lip.

"What's wrong?"

She hesitated. "Oren took that photo."

He gazed at her for a moment, then realization slowly dawned.

Of course. He should have guessed. He wanted to laugh.

"It's you, isn't it?" he asked. If it hadn't been for the heavy makeup and the difference in hair color, he'd have guessed right away.

The woman who haunted his dreams didn't just resemble Summer. She *was* Summer.

He watched now as Summer nodded. "Please don't tell anyone."

"What? Why?" He paused, then asked as suspicion dawned, "No one in your family knows?"

She nodded again. "I posed for Oren once as a favor in order to help him with his career, but only on the condition that he use a pseudonym for me and never publicly link me to the photos."

"So that's why the woman is identified as Daphne."

"Yes.

Another thought occurred, and he drew his brows together. "There aren't any nudes, are there?"

Her eyes widened. "What? No!"

"So what's the problem?"

Her face shuttered. "I just didn't want to cause my family any embarrassment."

"What's to be embarrassed about?" He frowned. "Are you sure your motivation was simply that you didn't want to embarrass your family? Or was this your little private act of rebellion against the strictures of being an Elliott?"

When she didn't answer, he said, "Let me guess. Striking provocative poses for an up-and-coming but unknown photographer didn't mesh well with the image of Summer Elliott as the oh-so-proper publishing heiress and Manhattan debutante."

"Oh, shut up."

He grinned. "Tsk, tsk. Not very polite."

"I'm glad you find this so amusing."

"In fact, I do," he concurred. "Amusing and fascinating. You see, I already own a photograph of Daphne, er, you."

She looked surprised. "You do?"

He nodded. "It's hanging in my home in Los Angeles. That's why I asked you that first night after the concert whether you'd done any modeling."

"I denied doing any because no one was supposed to know about it."

He grinned. "Caitlin, Daphne, Summer. Are there any other personas that I should know about?"

"Very funny."

He regarded her thoughtfully. "Daphne has darker hair, though."

"My hair was digitally enhanced in the photos to make it a couple of shades darker than its natural color."

"Ah." No wonder both Summer and Daphne called forth the song for him: they were one and the same person. In his mind's eye, he saw "Daphne at Play." The woman's face was heavily made-up, her body draped sensuously on a chaise longue.

"You know," he mused, "I love the photograph of you that I have back in L.A. It was the reason I was so dumbstruck when you walked into my dressing room after the concert."

"You do? You were?" She looked pleased, flattered, and—he hoped this wasn't just a figment of his fevered imagination—as if she wanted to jump his bones.

"Let's get out of here," he said huskily.

She nodded.

He wanted her badly. As he punched the button for the elevator, he just hoped he could hold out until they got back to the Waldorf. He didn't want to think of tomorrow's newspaper headlines if they got caught having sex in his car.

Before leaving the gallery, however, he stopped long enough to convince Oren to consider selling him the copyright to all the Daphne photos.

He'd pay whatever it took. If one photo of Daphne could stir his imagination, who knew what a roomful of photos would do for his creativity? And then, of course, there was the stimulating idea of possessing Summer's little secret.

Ten

Summer looked around Zeke's mansion again as she waited for him to return from running an errand. It was a bright Sunday morning, and she relished the mild southern California weather. She couldn't remember being happier.

After leaving the art gallery on Wednesday night, they'd wound up back at Zeke's hotel suite, where they'd made love until the early hours of the morning and then fallen asleep in each other's arms.

On Thursday, they'd dined with his parents, whom she'd found to be smart, witty and charming. Sort of, she thought with a smile, like their son.

And then, somehow, she'd let Zeke talk her into coming out to L.A. this weekend. She'd announced at work that she wouldn't be in on Friday, so the two of them had been able to fly out to the West Coast together.

Now, as she walked from room to room in Zeke's Beverly Hills mansion, she was struck anew by how impressive his estate was. When they'd arrived on Friday afternoon, he'd shown her around a bit, but she didn't have a chance to form more than a general impression. She'd seen that the landscaped grounds boasted an indoor pool, a tennis court and a guest cottage. The house itself, a two-story in the Spanish Mission style, had a red-tile roof, arched doorways and a wonderful veranda, where they'd dined their first night al fresco because of the unseasonably warm weather.

This morning she picked up details that she'd missed in her first walk-through. She loved the way his decor blended antiques of different periods for a look that was stately but still warm and welcoming.

Gram would have approved. She herself approved. Very much. His style reflected her own tastes.

As she walked to the back of the house, she couldn't help thinking that, so far, their time in L.A. had been idyllic. Yesterday she'd snapped photos of him shirtless, then he'd laughingly taken the camera from her and snapped pictures of her. They'd played tennis, then taken a dip in the pool, which had led to their making love in the pool house, despite her half-hearted protests that someone might stumble upon them. At night, they'd eaten dinner at the Hotel Bel-Air, which had one of the city's swankiest restaurants.

On top of it all, Zeke was having a subtle but sure influence on other aspects of her life. Her wardrobe had become sexier and more stylish—in no small part, she realized, because she wanted to entice him. And, of course, thanks to him, she was playing hooky from work—and liking it—for the first time in her life.

Summer stopped as she entered Zeke's music room, where, he'd told her, he liked to play and compose. She looked again at the photograph that hung over the mantel.

She remembered when Oren had taken that shot of her as Daphne, the Greek goddess. She'd been nervous because she'd felt as if she were rebelling, just as Zeke had guessed.

It gave her a thrill to think Zeke had seen "Daphne at Play," and known that he had to have it. It made her believe that it hadn't just been she who'd felt an instant connection, as if they'd known each other forever, when they'd met for the first time. It made her think that something significant had started that night—significant enough to necessitate breaking off her engagement to John.

"I see you've spotted the photo," said a voice behind her.

She turned from the photograph to face the man who was sauntering into the room.

"Hello, Marty," she said. She'd been introduced to Zeke's manager yesterday. He'd struck her as an experienced music-industry operator who always kept his eye on his client's interests and who'd perhaps seen too many rising music stars combust on their way to the top.

Marty stopped beside her. "You know, when Zeke told me that you'd walked into his dressing room back in New York, I thought, what an amazing coincidence."

She smiled. "Wasn't it?"

"And lucky, too. But then luck's always seemed to be on Zeke's side. His first album was released just when the public seemed to have a hankering for romantic and sexy ballads."

"I didn't know it was considered lucky that Zeke met me," she said, unable to keep from feeling flattered.

"He was going through a real dry spell as far as getting down songs for his next album. Sort of a writer's block." Marty nodded at the space over the mantel. "The photo was the one thing that could unblock him and get the creative juices flowing again." He looked back at her. "Of course, having you in the flesh has been even better."

Summer wondered uncomfortably if there was a double meaning in Marty's last words, but he just looked at her placidly. Surely he couldn't have meant "having her in the flesh" literally. Aloud, she said, "I didn't realize I was helping Zeke's creativity."

"Didn't you?" Marty returned, then nodded. "Yes, you're more or less his muse for the time being."

Something in Marty's tone gave her pause.

Marty looked from the photograph to her again. "You know, at first I was worried. A deep entanglement wouldn't be good for Zeke's career. Millions of women see him as a sex symbol."

She managed a nod of agreement. She wasn't sure where this conversation was heading.

"But then," Marty went on, "once Zeke explained his involvement with you was for, uh, artistic purposes, I realized there was nothing to worry about."

"I see." Summer felt a tightness growing and taking hold in the pit of her stomach.

Marty sighed. "Unfortunately, a celebrity of Zeke's caliber has an image to maintain and a publicity machine that needs to be fed—with the right kind of publicity, of course."

"Of course." She was beginning to dislike Marty, but then again, was she just blaming the messenger? Working at an entertainment magazine, she, more than most people, knew the truth in Marty's words about the nature of a celebrity's existence.

Zeke was at the top of his game. He was young, talented and blessed with movie-star good looks. As a sex symbol, it wouldn't be good for him to get deeply involved with someone or, heaven forbid, engaged or married at this point.

"You work for *The Buzz*, don't you?" Marty said. "Of course, you understand how these things work. Just in the last couple of days, I had to plant a story linking Zeke to a supermodel and then issue a non-denial to a competing newspaper. Zeke's got to stay in the public eye, and my job is to keep tongues wagging, but about the right type of stuff."

Summer nodded. She really needed for this conversation to end. She felt sick. She should have known someone like Zeke wouldn't have been attracted to someone like her unless there was an ulterior motive. They were…different.

How naive could she be? Very, she answered herself.

Aloud, she said, "Would you excuse me, Marty?" The comportment-school grad in her kicked in. Politeness under the most distressing situations. Especially in the most distressing situations. "I have a phone call to make." A little white lie, sparingly used, could rescue anyone from the worst circumstances.

"Of course," Marty said. "Enjoy the rest of your stay in L.A."

"Thank you," she managed, then turned and walked toward the door, her head held high and her back ramrod straight. A part of her couldn't shake the feeling, however, that she was fleeing…and Marty knew it.

* * *

"You're leaving?" Zeke asked in disbelief. "Why?"

He'd thought they'd agreed to fly back to New York City together on the redeye tomorrow night. He had a meeting to attend tomorrow morning with his talent agency in L.A., but then he'd be free to accompany her back to New York.

Instead, here she was packing and announcing she was leaving on an overnight flight tonight.

Summer tossed her bathing suit into her suitcase. "I decided I needed to get back. I have a job, remember? A job that I want to advance in."

He was distracted by the bathing suit. He remembered taking it off her yesterday and what had happened afterward.

"I know you have a job," Zeke said, forcing his gaze back to Summer, "but I thought we'd agreed to leave tomorrow night."

"I changed my mind," she said, continuing to pack.

"Damn it, Summer," he said, his patience finally snapping as he grabbed the skirt that she was about to toss into her luggage. "Would you look at me? What is this really about?"

Probably because she didn't have a choice, she stopped. After a moment, she said, "This weekend has been wonderful, but it's also made me realize we're two completely different people with two completely different lifestyles."

He just looked at her. What had happened? He thought they'd been heading toward…something.

She grabbed the skirt back from him and tossed it into the suitcase. "I need to get some perspective, and for *that,* I think there needs to be some space between us."

"Perspective? Perspective on what?" he asked, dumbfounded. A part of his mind understood what she was saying, but he just didn't want to believe it.

Usually, *he* was the one having to let the woman down easy. He'd never liked doing it, and had never boasted about the number of times that he'd had to do so, but it was just a fact of life, given who he was. There would always be women who were ready to appear on the arm of a rock star, however briefly.

He watched as Summer took a deep breath. "Our lives are totally different, Zeke. You tour a lot, and I'm committed to climbing the ladder at EPH."

"Are you?" he asked. "I've started to wonder, you know. You're a great photographer, and you have a real passion for it."

"Becoming a reporter at *The Buzz* is my goal," she said emphatically. "It's the reason I met you, remember?"

"I remember," Zeke said, "but I've also realized that EPH was your grandfather's dream. It doesn't have to be for all his kids and grandkids."

"I know, but it's been my dream for forever."

He wanted to say more, wanted to argue with her, but he decided it would be more productive to change tactics. "Look, even if EPH is what you want, that doesn't mean we can't be together."

"For how long?" she countered.

He had no answer to that. Marty's admonition sounded in his head: *Don't get serious with anyone.* It wouldn't be good for his career.

"I don't want the globe-trotting lifestyle," Summer continued, "and you're not ready to settle down."

What could he say to that? He hadn't really thought about where their relationship was heading. He'd just been happy to take each day as it came. That was how it had been in every past relationship.

Yet, Summer seemed ready to cut her losses now.

"You need to feed a voracious publicity machine," she went on. "You need to stay in the public eye with the right type of publicity, and that's not me. That's not what I want."

Again, he couldn't argue with her. In fact, she was sounding a lot like Marty with her harping on the re-quirements of his career.

He tried the only tactic that he had left. "Come on, Summer. You've come a long way from where you were just three weeks ago. You're finally breaking out of your shell. Don't back away now. Seize the opportunity."

"Maybe the shell is who I am," she said quietly,

"and you should stop kidding yourself or thinking I'm transforming into someone else."

She turned her back to go to the dresser and get more of her clothes, and Zeke knew that, from her perspective, the conversation was over. They were over.

"Summer."

"Hmm."

"Summer."

Summer swiveled around in her chair at work and noticed her uncle Shane lurking at the opening of her cubicle. She started guiltily. Ever since she'd left L.A. three days ago, she'd had trouble focusing on work. It was now Wednesday, and she was still trying to concentrate.

Shane rested his arm on top of the cubicle's partition. "Good news."

She could use some. "Oh?"

Shane grinned. "You're getting promoted. Next month, you'll be a reporter here at *The Buzz*."

She forced a smile, the news arousing mixed emotions. "Thanks."

"You came through for *The Buzz*, kid, with that interview with Zeke Woodlow. You've helped us keep up with the competition in this game that Granddad started, and you deserve to be rewarded."

In Summer's opinion, Shane had coped with Granddad's challenge better than most of the rest of the family. But then, Shane seemed to view the competition among EPH magazines as a game—a game that perhaps would be interesting and amusing to win.

Shane cocked his head to the side. "What's wrong? I thought you'd be elated about the promotion." He looked at her quizzically. "Isn't this what you've been gunning for?"

She had been. She'd come out and said so last year in her annual employee review. So, what was wrong with her?

For Shane's benefit, she tried a game smile. "Of course, I'm happy." *No, you're not.* "It's what I've always wanted." *Until now.* "I'm just trying to absorb it all. After all, I've been aiming for this promotion for a long time."

Shane nodded, then winked. "Great. We'll have a celebratory drink on Friday."

The staff of *The Buzz* sometimes converged at a nearby bar for TGIF—Thank God It's Friday—drinks, but this time Summer found it hard to work up any enthusiasm. "Thanks, Shane."

When her uncle had left, Summer found herself staring at her computer screen. She wished she could confide in Scarlet, but her sister had been distant and remote lately, not to mention rarely home. Summer couldn't help thinking Scarlet's behavior was due to her breaking up with John and hooking up with Zeke, though Scarlet had never come out and said as much.

She was still morose when she got home that night. As usual, Scarlet wasn't home when she got there, though Summer heard her come in after she'd gone to bed.

It had been three days without a word from Zeke. Summer knew she had no reason to expect him to call, but, perversely, she wanted him to.

After tossing and turning in bed without being able to sleep, she gave up in the early hours of the morning and went to sit on the couch in the living room, staring ahead as the city lights outside created a dim glow in the room.

She was so confused. Today, she'd hit another milestone in her five-year plan by getting her coveted promotion.

She should have been happy, ecstatic even, but she wasn't. She should have been celebrating with John, but she wasn't.

She remembered Zeke's words: *You can't live life by a neat plan.*

She mulled over what he'd said, and wondered if that's what she'd been doing. Had she been trying to make life nice and tidy when, by nature, it was messy and full of the unexpected?

She'd realized she was marrying John just because he fit in with her long-standing plans, but maybe he wasn't the only aspect of her life that she should have been questioning. Maybe trying to move up at *The Buzz* had become something she did unthinkingly, without examining why she was striving for it anymore.

What was it that Zeke had said? *Sometimes plans can get in the way of getting what you really want.*

What did Summer Elliott really want? She almost feared opening that door and finding out what lurked inside, but she forced herself to.

What did she want?

Just as Zeke had said, she was a far cry from the Summer of even a month ago. Gone were the twin sets and pearls and kitten heels. Today she'd gone to work dressed in a bottle-green V-neck top, a snug blazer that outlined her breasts, pants that rode low on her hips and black pumps. The look was sophisticated but soft. Thanks to several after-work shopping trips, her style wasn't Scarlet's, but neither was she the conservative retro chick that she'd been when dating John.

Will the real Summer Elliott please stand up? she thought wryly.

She closed her eyes and thought about the transformations of the past month. She let her mind loose, freed it to think about her most secret desires.

Release your inner goddess…. Release your inner goddess….

Scarlet's words came back to her.

She thought about what she really wanted and realized it wasn't being a reporter, or *The Buzz*, or even EPH. She'd enjoyed interviewing Zeke, but what made her happy was photography. She loved capturing the world around her with a camera.

She hadn't let herself seriously pursue photography because…well, because of fear. Fear that she'd never be good enough to be more than an amateur, and fear of family expectation. She'd assumed—more than been told—that she was expected to work at EPH, just like everyone else in the family did.

She wondered now whether she'd sold herself short. Where would Granddad have gotten if he'd been afraid to succeed in publishing? If he'd let himself be bound by the customary fields of work for the son of Irish immigrants?

What was it that Zeke had said? *EPH was your grandfather's dream. It doesn't have to be for all his kids and grandkids.*

Maybe she'd gone about it all wrong. Maybe remaining true to Granddad's example meant pursuing her own dream rather than her grandfather's.

She opened her eyes and exhaled. *Yes.*

She didn't know what she'd do yet, but she did know her future wasn't tethered to EPH or *The Buzz*. She wanted to find out how much talent she had as a photographer. She'd love to have the sort of gallery exhibit that Oren had had recently.

Zeke's words echoed in her head. *You've come a long way…. Don't back away now.*

Finally, she knew what he'd meant. It wasn't just about John or her love life. It was about her life. Period.

She felt a smile touch her lips. How many times tonight had she thought about what Zeke had said? She didn't care whether it was due to having a mother who was a psychologist, or because he was in tune with emotions because of his music, Zeke Woodlow had taught her a lot about herself.

Her smile widened. She'd learned something— something profound—from a bad-boy rock sensation.

And, with that thought came another.

Release your inner goddess…. Release your inner goddess….

Her inner goddess, she realized, wanted Zeke Woodlow.

Her heartbeat kicked up a notch. She not only wanted Zeke's, she loved Zeke.

He was smart and funny, and he made her a better person by challenging her. And they had amazing chemistry. Sure, she'd learned a lot from him in bed, but she'd learned even more out of it.

She didn't have to wonder whether she was being swayed by Zeke having been her first lover. Intuitively, she knew she'd never have had the same chemistry with John or any other man even if she'd gone ahead and slept with any of them.

It all made sense now. She loved Zeke.

Yes, his career would often put him on the road,

but it would make life with him an adventure. And if she was going to be a serious photographer, a career on the road might be ideal. She'd never lack for interesting subjects and scenery.

It no longer mattered to her that she wouldn't be getting married at twenty-six…or even in the foreseeable future. She realized that life couldn't be lived according to a neat plan.

What mattered to her was that she and Zeke were committed to seeing where things led between them. She knew he'd remain a heartthrob to his fans, but she also knew she could accept that—as long as he felt as strongly about her as she did about him.

That thought should have buoyed her. Instead, she slumped back against the sofa cushions. The problem was that three days ago, she'd kicked Zeke out of her life.

She looked at the glass clock on the end table. It was one in the morning in New York, but only ten in the evening in Los Angeles.

She could call him, but she'd much rather talk to him in person. Then she remembered Zeke had said he had a concert in Houston at the end of the month.

Picking up the phone again, she got in touch with the airline that she usually used.

She was going to Houston, and this time, thanks to *The Buzz*, she hoped to have a press pass to get backstage.

Eleven

Zeke strummed his guitar, played a few bars and paused to jot down some notes.

Then, becoming distracted again, he tossed aside his pencil.

Damn. It was no use.

Since Summer had left four days ago, he'd found it hard to concentrate.

It was now Thursday, and he was still in L.A. He looked around his music room. If time apart was what she wanted, then that was what he'd give her. Anyway, the truth was, he'd been hanging around Manhattan for the past month mostly to be near her, rather than for any pressing business reason.

He had the song down now, and it was about her. It had always been about her, he realized. In a fit of inspiration last weekend, before she'd left, he'd finally gotten the song down—lyrics, melody and all—during the small hours of the morning while she'd slept.

Too bad that now she was gone, his writer's block had returned with a vengeance. He was unable to make any progress on another song, his thoughts straying again and again to Summer.

At a sound from the doorway, he looked up. "Hey, Marty." He looked back down and experimentally played a few notes.

Marty walked into the room. "How's it going?" his manager said, adding, "The housekeeper let me in."

Zeke put the guitar aside and stood up from the couch. "I wasn't expecting you."

"It's sort of an impromptu visit."

"Can I get you anything?" he said. It was almost lunchtime.

"Just some iced tea, if you have it. I want to talk to you."

Zeke nodded. Marty only ever stopped by to talk business.

When they were seated at a table on the veranda, he with a beer and Marty with his iced tea, Zeke said, "So shoot."

"How's work on the next CD going?"

"It's going," he said. "Slowly, but it's going."

Marty nodded, looked off into the distance, and then back at him. "Look, Zeke, I want you to consider something and keep an open mind about it."

Zeke thought he could guess what Marty was going to say.

"For this next album, I was thinking we could have you do remakes of some classic songs, and even get you a little help with the songwriting on new material."

"Marty, no." He raked his hand through his hair. "You know writing songs is what I want to do, and I need to establish my credentials. Get a few more hits under my belt."

"Zeke, under your contract, you need to have another CD out next year."

"I'll make the deadline," he responded, "but then I'm committing myself to doing the songwriting for the Broadway musical that I've been approached about."

"What? Look, I thought we'd discussed this."

He gave Marty a steely look. "You work for me, Marty."

He rarely had to pull rank, but he did it now.

More and more, he and Marty were seeing his career in different terms, and Zeke wondered how much longer they'd be able to work together. In the past, Marty had steered him right in many ways, but this was a decision that he felt strongly about. It was a question of vision—vision about what to do with *his* life.

"Zeke, be reasonable. At the moment, you can't even seem to get started on the songs for your next release."

"I was doing fine until Summer left," he grumbled.

Marty sighed heavily. "For a while there, you really had me worried about this Elliott woman."

Zeke cocked his head, sensing they were getting into dangerous territory. "How so?"

"You seemed to be getting hung up on her," Marty said, adding, "We both know that getting serious about any woman would be bad for your image. Women love you, Zeke, because you're the sexy bad-boy rocker that their mothers always warned them about."

"What made you realize I wasn't hung up on her?" Zeke asked, keeping his voice even.

Marty shrugged. "You said it yourself. She was your muse. Or rather, her photo was, initially. She wasn't your usual type, but once I realized why you were hanging around her, it all made sense."

Zeke remembered Marty had stopped by on Sunday when he'd been out, and he started to form a hunch. He nodded and said, "Summer was really taken with the coincidence of my owning 'Daphne at Play.'"

"I'll bet," Marty responded. "It's not every day that a woman realizes she's the inspiration for a major rock sensation. Very flattering."

Zeke forced himself to nod placidly. "You know, I never did get around to telling her that part."

"Yeah," Marty said, "it seemed to come as a bit of a surprise when I mentioned it to her."

"And did you also mention she should be flattered?" he asked, his voice too quiet.

Marty held up his hands. "Hey, Zeke, look—" He stopped and looked around. "Where is she, by the way? I was surprised when you left a message with my secretary saying you wouldn't be returning to New York on Monday like you'd planned."

"Summer's gone back to New York." Zeke stood. "And you're leaving."

Marty looked up at him uncomprehendingly for a second, until an astounded expression crossed his face. "What? Why? Do you have an appointment to keep somewhere?"

Zeke realized Marty figured he must be joking, but this was no joke. "You need to leave, Marty, before I give in to the urge to deck you." He added, "Believe it or not, I'd hate the bad publicity as much as you would."

Marty wiped his lips with his napkin before standing up. "When you've calmed down, you know where to reach me."

"I'm as calm as I'll ever be," Zeke replied. "What exactly did you say to Summer?"

Marty eyed him. "Is it my fault you didn't mention to her it was her photo that got you hot and bothered?"

Zeke waited, holding his temper in check.

Marty finally shook his head. "I pointed out the

obvious, including the requirements of your career right now." He perked up. "I planted a story about you and that hot Czech model in the press this week. Did you catch it? Nice touch, eh?"

Zeke shook his head. "You're just not getting it, Marty."

"Getting what?"

"For a while, I've thought that the two of us weren't on the same wavelength as far as my career was concerned. I chose to ignore the feeling—until now." He looked the other man in the eye. "You're fired, Marty."

"What?" Marty blustered. "You can't fire me. You need me. I'll sue your pants off."

"Take it to my lawyer," Zeke said coldly. "I think our contract allows me to pay you off to dump you. It's a price I'm willing to pay."

"This over a nice piece of ass?" Marty sneered.

Zeke didn't need to think about it. He threw Marty out on his ear.

Much later, Zeke sat in his living room gazing sightlessly at the television.

Marty had echoed some of the same things that Summer had said on Sunday: she wasn't his usual type, and they were different in a lot of ways. And, yeah, he couldn't deny that he did have his career to consider.

He wondered, though, how much of what Summer

had said was due to her reaction to Marty's words and how much was due to her own feelings coming to light.

Zeke's jaw tightened. He couldn't lose Summer. He'd never felt this way about a woman before. Unfortunately, that also meant he was in uncharted territory about how to make things right.

When the phone rang and he heard a familiar voice, he was only too happy for the distraction. Minutes later, when he hung up, he knew what he had to do.

Zeke's concert was the same as the first two she'd attended. At least this time, Summer thought ruefully, she knew what to expect.

She was surrounded by thousands of Zeke Woodlow fans, all gyrating and bumping and singing and hollering their way through Zeke's repertoire of songs.

This time she was dressed more appropriately, too. She wore hip-hugging jeans and a deep scoop-neck top.

She looked up at Zeke on stage, and her heart swelled.

He strode around the stage as if he owned it—the mark of any great performer. He picked up his guitar, he sang along with one of his backup musicians, and he egged on his fans with teasers. And always he was in sync with his audience.

She hungrily took in every inch of him. He looked gorgeous. It had been almost a week since they'd parted, and she couldn't believe how much she'd missed him.

She rubbed damp palms against her jeans as she mouthed the words to one of Zeke's most popular songs.

She was a little nervous about the reception that she'd receive from Zeke, but she was going for broke. He was the man she loved, and she wasn't going to let him walk out of her life without telling him so.

Once or twice, she thought she caught Zeke staring straight at her in the audience, his gaze intense and magnetic. But she dismissed the thought as fanciful. There were thousands of people in the audience, and though she had one of the better seats, the lighting was dim and she was several rows back and off to one side.

Besides, if there was one thing she'd come to know about Zeke, it was that he was able to make every audience member feel connected to him.

She couldn't wait to get backstage at the end of the concert. This time, thanks to some last-minute wrangling and imploring Shane to pull strings, she had a good seat *and* a press pass.

Of course, she'd had to explain to Shane why she couldn't just approach Zeke for access, and the truth—well, some of it—had come tumbling out of her. She'd admitted she and Zeke had recently become romantically involved.

Shane hadn't been too happy at the news, given

-that it made it awkward that *The Buzz* was publishing an interview with Zeke under her name, but he'd eventually waved her off, especially when she'd told him what she was considering in terms of her career.

He'd just looked at her and sighed. "Ah, Summer," he said. "You're the last Elliott that I'd have expected to even think about doing something like this."

"I know," she'd said somewhat guiltily. She knew that, no matter how lightheartedly Shane had taken Granddad's challenge up to now, he probably wouldn't mind winning, and she'd just announced a potential setback for *The Buzz* in the race among EPH magazines.

Shane had finally waved her out of his office. "Okay, kid, go get your man, and good luck to you. Never say that I stood in the way of true love."

"Thanks, Uncle Shane!" she'd said gratefully, then kissed him on the cheek before beating a hasty retreat.

And now, here she was at Zeke's concert, the moment of truth soon to be upon her.

On stage, Zeke flashed a grin at the audience as he took a break between songs. "I've got a surprise for you."

The crowd hooted and hollered.

"Are you ready?"

The audience responded even more loudly.

Zeke slung the strap of his guitar over his neck.

"For the grand finale, I'm going to unveil a new song just for you."

The crowd went wild as the music struck up.

Zeke played some notes experimentally. "It's called 'Days of Sunshine and Summer.'"

Summer froze in mid-clap. He didn't... He hadn't... The title was just a coincidence, she told herself. Surely, he meant the season, and not the woman. Not her. Surely, he hadn't written a song about their breakup—a song that he was about to play for the thousands of people around her.

Zeke nodded to the band behind him, then launched into a ballad of heated intensity about unexpected love. The song was a play on the word *summer*, so that it seemed as if the woman that he sang about was the same as the season: hot, bright and uplifting. "Summer she called to me/Sunny and inviting as a beautiful day," he sang.

Summer held her breath. The song didn't contain a word about heartbreak or betrayal or breakup. Its mood was upbeat and inspiring. And, if the words of the song were true, then Zeke loved summer—loved *her*.

The song brought tears to her eyes. There was no way that Zeke could know she was in the audience. Had he just used their romance—however brief it had been—to fuel his songwriting? Or, as she wanted to believe, were the words of his song true and heartfelt?

When the final notes of the song drifted away, Zeke seemed to look straight at her, and this time Summer could swear she wasn't wrong.

Moving to the microphone, he said, "Everyone, I'd like you to meet Summer."

Before she could blink, a spotlight shone on her. Under other circumstances, Summer was sure she would have reacted like a deer caught in headlights. But right now, her gaze was captured and held by the look on Zeke's face.

Zeke held out his hand to her. "Summer, come on up here."

Crazy as it was, it seemed that only she and Zeke existed, and her feet impelled her toward him.

She walked up onto the stage, the security guards making way for her. Her gaze was fixed on Zeke, the periphery of her vision a blur.

When she finally reached him, he took hold of her hand. The look on his face stole her breath. It was heated and adoring, and it contained just a touch of mischief.

He cast a sidelong look at the audience. "Sorry to embarrass you like this, sweetheart," he said, sounding not the least bit apologetic.

The crowd laughed.

"What are you doing?" she whispered.

He gazed into her eyes and whispered back, "Do you love me?"

"Yes," she answered. She didn't have to think about it.

To the audience, he said, "She loves me."

In response, there was whooping and laughter and clapping.

"You crazy man," she said, trying to keep her voice low enough not to be picked up by the mike in front of him. "What are you doing? Your career—"

He silenced her with a passionate kiss that had the crowd clapping and laughing some more.

Summer clung to him. The kiss quickly brought forth the electricity that always crackled between them.

When he lifted his head and let her go, she watched in disbelief as he sank down on one knee and pulled a ring from his pocket, his eyes never leaving hers.

"Summer, I love you. Will you marry me?"

Her hands flew over her mouth, and tears welled in her eyes.

There were several calls from the audience of "Say yes!" And this time Summer knew there wasn't a doubt in her heart.

Lowering her hands, she cried, "Yes!"

Zeke beamed at her, his face breaking into a grin.

He took her trembling hand and slipped onto her finger an antique band with a diamond flanked by two emeralds. Then he stood up, gathered her into his arms and bent her backward for a deep kiss.

When they broke apart, he flashed her a grin. "I hope you don't mind the PDAs."

"The new Summer Elliott likes public displays of affection a lot," she responded breathlessly.

Minutes later, in the privacy of Zeke's dressing room, Summer found herself in Zeke's arms.

"How did you even know I was in the audience?" she asked, resting her hands on his chest.

Zeke nibbled at her lips. "Mmm…Shane told me."

Her eyes widened. "He did?" Because her voice sounded squeaky, she tried again. "I mean, he did?" She didn't know whether to thank her uncle or not.

Laughter lurked in Zeke's eyes. "How else do you think he got his hands on a press pass and a last-minute ticket for one of the better seats in the house? The concert's been sold out for a while."

Summer's eyes narrowed with suspicion. "What did he say, exactly?"

"Exactly? I don't remember."

She swatted him playfully. "Try."

A smile hovered at the corners of his lips. "He didn't say too much. He just said you were desperately looking for a ticket and a press pass in order to get backstage to see me." He added, "Given how things had ended between us, Shane's call was enough to make me hope you weren't showing up just to put the final nail in the coffin of our relationship."

"He used the word *desperate?*"

Zeke laughed. "You look like you're not sure whether to give Shane an earful."

"Mmm-hmm."

"I'm sure he was just trying to help, and, you know, everything turned out well in the end." He gave her a quick kiss. "Just out of curiosity, though, if I hadn't called you on stage and proposed—"

"Yes, that was a surprise. In front of all those people, Zeke!"

He grinned unapologetically. "But if I hadn't done it, what were you planning to do?"

"Get backstage, lock you in your dressing room and refuse to let you out until you realized our relationship deserved a real chance."

"I've known that all along."

"But Marty said—"

"I know what Marty said. Forget it." For a second, Zeke looked fierce.

"You do? How do you know what he said?"

Zeke relaxed his hold on her. "He stopped by the house on Thursday, and his conversation with you came up." Zeke shrugged. "Let's just say Marty and I had a parting of the ways."

Summer's eyes widened. "What? Zeke, no. Not because of me."

"It wasn't just because of you, Summer, though that brought it to a head. Marty and I have been drifting in different directions. He thought I should concentrate on being a sex-symbol rock star, but songwriting is my real passion."

Zeke stepped back, letting her go. "After this international tour is over at the end of the year, I'm settling down in one place for a while." His lips turned up at one side. "I guess New York City is as good a place as any."

She moved toward him. "Zeke, you don't have to do that on my account. I know I said I didn't want to be on the road all the time, but—" she bit her lip "—that's because I was so hurt when I thought you were just using me to get through your songwriting block."

His smile widened. "Too late. I've signed up to do the songwriting for a musical that's being put together by one of the biggest producers on Broadway. That'll be my next big commitment after I fulfill my contract by recording another CD."

She clapped her hands. "Oh, Zeke! I'm so happy for you!"

He shrugged. "Writing for the Broadway show is an offer that I've been toying with for a while. I was approached about it a couple of months ago, but Marty hated the idea, and at the time, I wasn't prepared to part ways with him."

His gaze softened as he looked down at her. "Besides, doing Broadway will give me some time closer to my parents. And," he teased, "I'm assuming you'll want me in New York for the wedding."

"Of course!" She gazed down at the ring that he'd given her and said, "The ring is perfect."

"I'm glad you like it. I thought you'd like something old and unique. The emeralds remind me of your Irish eyes."

She looked up at him. "I didn't think you were ready to settle down."

"I realized I was waiting for the right woman to come along," he said thoughtfully. "The rest was just a public image carefully cultivated by Marty supposedly for the sake of my career."

She nodded, her heart catching on the words *the right woman.*

"It's true that the photo of Daphne was my songwriting inspiration after a dry spell," he said. "In fact, the photo inspired 'Beautiful in My Arms.'"

"I love that song!" she said. She loved it even more now that she knew the song was about Daphne—or, rather, her.

"Yeah, well," he said, looking amused, "I composed it after a particularly hot dream about Daphne—er, you."

She laughed.

"Of course, after that," he went on, "I couldn't get another song written—until I met you. I'd been dreaming about another song but I couldn't seem to hold on to it when I woke up. But when I was around you, the song started coming to me, and last weekend I finally wrote 'Days of Sunshine and Summer.'"

His eyes held hers. "You may have started out as my muse, but you became so much more than that."

"Oh," she said, caught by the look on his face.

His hands clasped her loosely around the waist. "Given the way the fans reacted to the marriage proposal tonight, I've got to wonder whether Marty was a little narrow-minded about what was good for my career."

She laughed. "How ironic."

He looked confused. "What is?"

"That just when you're ready to settle down, I'm planning to give notice to Shane that I'm taking a leave of absence from *The Buzz* and EPH—probably in anticipation of my eventual resignation. In fact, I've already hinted as much to him."

A look of surprise crossed his face. "What?"

"How else am I supposed to follow you as you travel the world?"

"Aw, Summer." He kissed her, and when the kiss threatened to become deeper, he pulled back and looked at her soberly. "I hope you're not taking the leave just because of me."

She shook her head. "No. It's for me, too. I finally decided to give myself permission to pursue what I really want. You…and photography."

"Good for you."

"Thanks. I'm going to freelance, which should give me maximum flexibility for planning a wedding and spending time with you." She shrugged. "Maybe some of my work will end up in EPH's magazines. I think Shane would be open to acquiring some of my photos."

"Sure. I know I would."

"You're not exactly unbiased," she joked, then added more somberly, "I wonder how Granddad will take the news."

"Something tells me, better than you think."

Summer looked at him in surprise. "What makes you say that?"

"It would be hypocritical of him to do otherwise, don't you think? After all, he went off and pursued his dream."

"Mmm." It was only recently that she'd come to look at matters the same way herself.

"You know," Zeke continued, "I wondered whether working your way up at EPH was another way of pleasing your family, just like getting engaged to John was."

"It may have been," she said. "My grandparents sort of stepped into the shoes of my parents after the plane crash. Instead of trying to please parents, I was trying to please grandparents."

Zeke nodded. "Maybe your preoccupation with planning stems from the plane crash. You know, it's an attempt to impose order and predictability on life, which you learned at an early age can be surprising and scary."

His insightfulness surprised her, though she supposed it shouldn't anymore.

"Anyway," he said teasingly, "I guess you wound up sticking to your five-year plan after all."

"What do you mean?"

"You'll be getting married by twenty-six."

When she realized he was right, she wanted to laugh.

He pulled her closer. "Tell me again that you love me," he murmured.

"Every day," she said just before his lips met hers.

Then there was no more talking. Instead, she gave herself up to the happiness that she'd discovered in his arms.

* * * * *

If you enjoyed what you just read,
then we've got an offer you can't resist!

Take 2 bestselling
love stories FREE!
Plus get a FREE surprise gift!

Clip this page and mail it to Silhouette Reader Service™

IN U.S.A.	IN CANADA
3010 Walden Ave.	P.O. Box 609
P.O. Box 1867	Fort Erie, Ontario
Buffalo, N.Y. 14240-1867	L2A 5X3

YES! Please send me 2 free Silhouette Desire® novels and my free surprise gift. After receiving them, if I don't wish to receive anymore, I can return the shipping statement marked cancel. If I don't cancel, I will receive 6 brand-new novels every month, before they're available in stores! In the U.S.A., bill me at the bargain price of $3.80 plus 25¢ shipping and handling per book and applicable sales tax, if any*. In Canada, bill me at the bargain price of $4.47 plus 25¢ shipping and handling per book and applicable taxes**. That's the complete price and a savings of at least 10% off the cover prices—what a great deal! I understand that accepting the 2 free books and gift places me under no obligation ever to buy any books. I can always return a shipment and cancel at any time. Even if I never buy another book from Silhouette, the 2 free books and gift are mine to keep forever.

225 SDN DZ9F
326 SDN DZ9G

Name	(PLEASE PRINT)	
Address	Apt.#	
City	State/Prov.	Zip/Postal Code

Not valid to current Silhouette Desire® subscribers.

Want to try two free books from another series?
Call 1-800-873-8635 or visit www.morefreebooks.com.

* Terms and prices subject to change without notice. Sales tax applicable in N.Y.
** Canadian residents will be charged applicable provincial taxes and GST.
  All orders subject to approval. Offer limited to one per household.
  ® are registered trademarks owned and used by the trademark owner and or its licensee.

DES04R   ©2004 Harlequin Enterprises Limited

They're tall, dark…and ready to marry!

If you love reading about our sensual Italian men, don't delay.
Look out for the next story in this great miniseries!

PUBLIC WIFE,
PRIVATE MISTRESS
by Sarah Morgan

Only Anastacia, Rico Crisanti's estranged wife,
can help his sister. In public she'll be a perfect
wife and in private, a slave to his passion.
But will her role as Rico's wife last?

On sale April 2006.

It's a
SUMMER OF SECRETS

Expecting
Lonergan's Baby
(#1719)

by

MAUREEN CHILD

He'd returned only for the summer…until a
passionate encounter with a sensual stranger
has this Lonergan bachelor contemplating
forever…and fatherhood.

Don't miss the SUMMER OF SECRETS trilogy,
beginning in April from Silhouette Desire.

On sale April 2006

Available at your favorite retail outlet!

COMING NEXT MONTH

#1717 THE FORBIDDEN TWIN—Susan Crosby
The Elliotts
Seducing your twin sister's ex-fiancé by pretending to be her…
not the best idea. Unless he succumbs.

#1718 THE TEXAN'S FORBIDDEN AFFAIR—
Peggy Moreland
A Piece of Texas
He swept her off her feet, then destroyed her. Now he wants her
back!

#1719 EXPECTING LONERGAN'S BABY—
Maureen Child
Summer of Secrets
He was home just for the summer—until a night of explosive
passion gave him a reason to stay.

#1720 THEIR MILLION-DOLLAR NIGHT—
Katherine Garbera
What Happens in Vegas…
This businessman has millions at stake in a deal but one woman
has him risking scandal and damning the consequences!

#1721 BABY, I'M YOURS—Catherine Mann
It was only supposed to be a weekend affair, then an unexpected
pregnancy changed all of the rules.

#1722 THE SOLDIER'S SEDUCTION—
Anne Marie Winston
She thought the man who'd taken her innocence was gone
forever…until he returned home to claim her—and the daughter
he never knew existed.

SDCNM0306